Sheldon Shags A Shoggoth

&

Other Racy and Awkward Fantasy Tales

Ezra Owain

This book is for adults.

Specifically, adults into weird shit. It contains graphic sex, including sex with sapient non-humans (i.e. monsterfucking), various gender pairings, and elements of BDSM.

ISBN 979-8-9913181-2-9 (Paperback)

ISBN 979-8-9913181-3-6 (eBook)

Contents

*To my spouse and family, for always telling me
to go for it, even when it wasn't their thing*

*To all my wonderful beta readers and writing
buddies*

To Dr Chuck Tingle, who shows us the way

Love Is Real. Be the Change You Wish to See.

Baruch HaShem.

I had a strange series of dreams in the week before the Anomaly. Strange by normal human standards at least, strange to me at the time.

I'd wake up with the sensation of something heavy pressing down upon me, rub my eyes, and see the demon lying on top of me. That wasn't the weird part.

Some nights it took the form of a bearded incubus with big sexy horns; other nights a pert-breasted succubus with little fangs and a sleek tail; other nights, not woman or man, but an eldritch monster swimming with duplicate body parts and hybrid appendages. But that wasn't the weird part, either. I happen to be very queer and very into monster erotica.

What's odd was in these dreams I had a big, beautiful penis, and the demon would be riding it, and I could swear it was my very own flesh. (Oh, and for some reason they always offered me orange juice after.) Back in high school I'd had plenty of dreams where I had a dick. But I'd found a lot of community since then, especially here in gay hippy Ithaca. I had gotten pretty comfortable with the fact my dick was a rainbow-colored 7 inch silicone dildo. I'd learned to manage the dysphoria around having a front hole. I'd come to terms with my oversized clit, which had always been visually neither here nor there; and my little round breasts passed for man-boobs now after years of T.

The night before the Anomaly, my sleep was deep and, to my memory, undisturbed. I'd chalked my dreams up to a recent change in meds. It made sense they'd go away as I adjusted. Truth be told, there had also been a noticeable uptick in intrusive thoughts, but I was coping, and that night I was pleased with myself. I'd done everything I could to beef up my support system in the pandemic. Zoom calls with friends, my therapist once a week. And in a few days my BFF, Sid, was coming over, after an unfortunate delay due to covid exposure.

The next day was an ordinary, quiet November day at the little farm on the snow-covered hill. I'd made a mutually beneficial arrangement to watch the farmhouse, since the Cornell campus was shut down for this semester and very likely the next. Zayde was weathering the pandemic at my sister's place in LA (another little piece of my support system was constant cute photos of my nieces on Snapchat), and what little work the farm itself needed this time of year was mostly left to contractors, who I didn't have to interact with. So it was quiet here, and it was quiet as a mouse down in East Ithaca, with the notable exception of the high-energy sciences laboratory. That lay a scant half-mile away at the foot of the hill. Coming back from my walk along the creek that afternoon, I could just hear the faint hum of transformers.

Because it was so quiet, it came as especially startling when it happened. I had just finished making dinner—tofu with black bean sauce, if memory serves—so I was doing dishes right in front of the kitchen window. A blue flash in the periphery of my sight left a ghostly impression, and then a white flash. Every light in the house flickered as I raced to the dining room to see what in hell was going on. An unearthly screech came ripping up the hill, followed by a BANG like lightning at close range. I made it to the big bay window.

The upper east wing of the lab was belching flames of an unholy crimson.

They danced hypnotically, and when I say that I do mean it. I must have zoned out for a couple minutes. Then I snapped back to attention; I could have sworn I saw a red streak fly away from the building just then, in the direction of the woods south of here. It was already gone from the corner of my eye, though.

As I stood there alert but confused, a procession of emergency vehicles began to arrive. Fire trucks, then police, then a trio of unmarked black SUVs. The DoD protecting its research investments, I thought. In the half hour or so that I stood watching, they got the fire mostly under control. But those top two levels of the east wing were donezo. At last I dragged myself away; it was time to eat my food before it was room temperature, and give Sid a call. This shit was unnerving.

I slept fitfully that night. No dreams of the demon, but plenty of dreams of crimson infernos, of me with different parts, extra parts, suffused with unearthly red aura, falling through holes in spacetime and drifting between far-flung worlds, where utterly alien creatures nursed unspeakable desires...

It was close to noon the next day when I finally rolled out of bed and into my signature gay-farmer overalls. I went about my routines in my quiet outskirt of my quiet town, but the absence of electrical hum out on the perimeter was surprisingly loud in my head. I felt dim and inscrutable foreboding.

Several hours, a delicious plate of leftovers and a generous dab later, I was huddled by the space heater upstairs, reading smut on the iPad. Tuesday night was 'date night', and I was determined not to let mere malaise stand in its way. See, I learned the hard way as a young queer man that the most important romantic and sexual relationship I can have—the one person I can always count on to love and respect me and bring me pleasure—is myself.

For a long time I didn't believe such a relationship was possible, let alone deserved. That got me into a lot of un-fun situations. I found myself in bed with homophobes, transphobes, chasers, and all manner of ignorant lazy jerks. If they weren't fetishizing my ambiguity, they were doing their damnedest to ignore my masculinity, presuming access to my shallow little front hole. G-d forbid they should ask first what *I* needed. So when I realized I could fuck myself ten times better than any of them, and at last began this relationship, I swore I would cherish it and keep it special. Thus, date night.

I lay on my back in the dimly lit bed with knees spread wide, wearing my plastic dick with a small vibrator tucked in the harness pocket. I was fucking my ass with a tentacle dildo I'd recently bought on Etsy. Unfortunately, I hadn't gotten very far into the main event when I was interrupted by a crash from outside, from the general direction of the sheds. I tensed from surprise and the dildo shot out halfway to the end of the bed. I sighed, hurriedly threw off the hardware and threw on sweats, and ran outside with a flashlight. I figured it was wild animals trying to get into the storehouse. Wouldn't be the first time.

But when I got to the sheds, there was no sign anything had happened at all. Windows and doorlocks were intact. All was quiet. Too quiet. I came back around in sight of the house, and just then, I shuddered. Again I could've sworn something had streaked across my field of vision. I looked toward the house, and saw nothing. Yet something set my heart pounding fruitlessly against the walls of its cage.

I was alone. No one to see me act like a silly child, so I abandoned pretense and sprinted to the door.

Thirty yards, nothing.

Twenty yards, still nothing.

Ten yards... a diffuse red glow rose up out of the bushes. Conscious thought lagged behind. I was running on adrenaline and reflex. A moment later, I was at the door, throwing it wide, almost forgetting to shut it, slamming it, trying the lock, omigod why isn't it locking, holy shit it isn't shut all the way, holy shit there's an arm in the door, a clawed hand shit shit shit...

I opened the door and slammed it repeatedly. Terrifying awareness began to seep in. The arm in the door broke off and clattered to the floor, and finally the door closed and the lock clicked.

LET US IN! came a voice within my own head. A talon twitched uselessly on the floor a moment, and t hen... rancid red light began pouring in under the door, suffusing the severed limb with monstrous essence. I bounded up the stairs. But just as I was bouncing off the wall at the first landing, I heard, STOP, and for some reason I did.

Staring down from the landing I finally found my voice: "What in hell are you?"

HELL? The voice snorted and laughed. A CRUDE TITLE FOR THE OUTER REALM, BUT IT WILL DO. YES. WE ARE OF THE REALM.

"Demon, what do you want?"

WHAT DO *YOU* WANT? IT WAS YOU WHO CALLED TO US.

"Called you? How?!" As I watched, the arm became whole again, and then a hulking, misshapen thorax growing outward and upward. And another arm. And another. All suffused with crimson glow.

WE WERE DRAWN TO YOUR DREAMS. OF EMBODIMENT, OF AFFIRMATION. OF LIVING AS YOU PICTURE YOURSELF.

"Wait. That was... you?"

YES.

"You came to me in my dreams, three versions of you, and you–you seduced me. You fucked me good and hard."

WAS THAT WRONG? WE ARE ACADEMICALLY CURIOUS WHETHER THAT WAS WRONG.

Such was the pull of the Anomaly's words in my head that I forgot fear, drawn into the conversation.

"Honestly? No, I thought it was hot as hell. Although, now it has me a bit fucked up. Like I must still be dreaming somehow."

OF ALL THE SAPIENT RACES WE'VE MET, ONLY HUMANS HAVE THIS UNFORTUNATE CONFUSION ABOUT WHICH REALM THEY'RE IN.

"I'm pretty sure this is not a dream. Where I am right now has none of the features of my dreams. I'm dressed normal, I look normal. I'm not sporting that dream peen."

TRUE.

"And yet, you're here. It doesn't work like that. Monsters from my dreams aren't supposed to just show up in the real world."

NORMALLY, NO. THE OUTER REALM AND YOURS DO NOT TOUCH, EXCEPT IN DREAMS. BUT THEN FOOLISH HUMANS MADE A SMALL HOLE IN REALITY. THEY DO NOT EVEN REALIZE WHAT THEY'VE DONE. BUT WE DID.

"Convenient. And you're offering me this embodiment? You would change my body in exchange for what, my soul? My servitude?" Terror was still floating in the back of my mind, not forgotten. It noticed first that the formless was taking form, a disorderly heap of extra arms and faces and things less human-like. More importantly, a form with two legs. Legs that were testing themselves out. Legs that were ready to move.

NOT EXACTLY. YOU HUMANS AND YOUR MYTHS. WOULD YOU BELIEVE THAT WE ARE SIMPLY PLEASED TO HELP WHEN WE HAVE THE MEANS?

"Call me a skeptic." I tried to keep my voice steady. The entity was slowly stepping forward.

WELL. IF TRANSACTION IS WHAT YOU UNDERSTAND, THERE *IS* SOMETHING WE REQUIRE.

"What? Sex?" The Anomaly stood silently at the foot of the stairs now, either lost in thought or preoccupied with working its newly formed body parts. This body had several misshapen faces still trying to arrange themselves, trying to figure out how to speak. Finally one of them coughed, took several ragged breaths, and said in an androgynous rasp,

"Yessss. Hah. Sexsss. Your, hah, waking, hah, flesh."

I was speechless.

"It's been a, hah, long time, hah, you see."

The Anomaly was coming up the stairs slowly now, and I still stood at the landing, transfixed by what I was hearing. Fear and arousal mixed with utter shock at the proposition. Here was a real life monster, the very one from my dreams; and now as then, its seven arms and legs sported an intimidating variety of digits, pincers, suckers and more. Eyes winked where they shouldn't. Fanged mouths licked themselves. Orifices puckered in and out of existence. Thick black hair covered what seemed to be the groin, but its sway hinted at more fun surprises.

"I'm... not saying no, but I have questions. How can I trust you?"

"Hah. You can, trust us or not. Hah. If we wanted a, hah, victim, we could have taken, anyone. Hah. We

"Yes. Yes, that is perfect."

"First door on the left, thanks. Um. Ana. There's something I have to tell you."

"You need not, worry, about the details of your anatomy. Not with us." As they spoke, Ana laid me down like the gentlest of human lovers, and gave my stomach an oddly reassuring thump with their squid-like foot-pod. The sucker-covered arm that supported my back now wrapped around my underboobs.

"I just generally don't use the front hole. Okay?"

"Of course. And these?" The face I thought of as Ana was smiling placidly at me and my little breasts. The face growing out of their chest, meanwhile, was examining my strap-on with a quizzical frown.

"Those are fair game. Oh, wow." I shuddered as they traced my areola. Another arm wasted no time in finding my clit. Hard edged little suckers and drooling taste bud-like projections grasped and licked at me, sending a stream of airy tingles and flickering pleasure flames up my spine. After several delightful minutes, they firmed their grip and began to rock back and forth, pushing and pulling at my bits much like a hu-man hand.

"Oh God, I'm gonna come soon."

"Yessss." They smiled broadly, and then with three of their arms, flipped me over onto my hands and knees as casually as I might have flipped a flapjack on the stove. I spread my legs and approvingly backed into them, and reached back with one hand to hold their arm. The rocking got faster, and the flames licked hotter until I was right at the edge of climax.

"Yesss, come for us." I could feel the mattress shift under Ana's weight as they positioned themself behind me, and then, I was startled by warm slick wetness pressing against my ass.

It is amazing how much a tentacle with its finger-like tip can feel like a tongue. Both are essentially long muscles anchored to nothing, able to move around and change shape while maintaining constant volume. The tentacle licked all around the rim of my asshole, one direction than the other, and I careened over the edge into orgasm land. I could feel my engorged clitoris shuddering with every spasm, and slickness continuing to leak from around my front hole.

Then just as my trembling subsided and my muscles began to relax, the tongue-like pod began to narrow and thrust itself little by little inside my ass. Here comes the main act. How could a night like this not involve a little ass probing?

"Oh, fuck!"

I felt the fullness inside me. I'd never been penetrated so rapidly and with such grace. There was no pain, and I realized with a shiver that it was because the pod didn't have to press its bulk through my butthole. It deformed itself to be finger-thin, slipped through, and then reinflated itself. When I clenched up, it didn't resist, it squashed down to almost nothing and waited for me to relent. Gradually I eased into relaxation and the stalk expanded.

Soon, I could feel Ana hunched over me. Their one human hand pressed down on the small of my back for support as the footpod thrust in and out of my ass. One arm still wrapped my chest, and one enveloped my clit and worked it like the head of a cock. I growled with pleasure. Already I was building up to a second orgasm.

"This is lovely. But what can I do for *you*?"

"All of this, is for me," they said. "I can taste your pleasure, hah, and mine."

"Isn't there something *selfish* you'd like?"

"We could... sample your pain, as well..."

Gently the tentacle withdrew from my ass. There was an audible *swish*... and a shock of pain as the pod flattened itself into a paddle and crashed against the back of my right thigh. Those chitinous little suckers that seemed so innocuous could really bite when fully exposed.

I cried out, in spite of myself. They paddled me again and again, hitting one butt cheek then the other, as air hissed between my gritted teeth. The sting it left was exquisite. I'm not a heavy pain bottom, so this was a little out of my comfort zone; but they managed to keep back from the edge of what I could handle. And their deft touch on my bits had me wanting to sink into, not run from, the experience.

"You're, hah, quiet." Ana was bent over me, so close that I could feel the breath of their speech on my neck.

"I'm good. Hnngh!" Sharp teeth sank into the meat of my shoulder, and the pod slipped back into my ass. Again and again I felt the icy bites—carefully measured to only just break the skin. I could still feel pain in my cheeks. A single drop of blood ran cold and wet down my back and ass. But beneath the skin, hot white light was spreading through my entire abdomen, from a focal point at the encircled clitoris.

This wasn't some humdrum little orgasm coming. This was Loma Prieta, this was Krakatoa, this was Chixulub.

"Oh god..."

I gripped the headboard with white knuckles and I screamed. Every clench of my pelvic muscles pulled the stiffened pod inside me, pressing it against the tender places. I squirted hard, and it splashed off the arm of my monstrous companion and onto my calves.

"Yesss. The power."

My legs gave out. I ground out the last of my orgasm in a trembling heap on the soaked sheets.

"I think... I need a minute," I said, before I rolled over and passed out.

When I awoke, I didn't know what time it was. The unmistakable smell of breakfast impinged upon my nose. I looked left, and saw a plate of fried eggs and a glass of OJ on the nightstand; and behind them, a red blur that my brain vaguely registered as the Anomaly.

"Eat," they said. "You need replenishment. We may have, ah, used you, too aggressively."

"You cooked?"

"Unfertilized dinosaur ova, sterilized by fire. We admire such symbiotic transfer of energy, given your species' penchant for destruction."

"Yeah, I'm a child of hippie vegetarians. I don't sup-pose you know how to make coffee?"

They did not. I dragged myself out of bed and trudged downstairs, despite feeling slightly hung over. Sex with a demon really does take a lot out of you.

When I returned, I realized something about Ana was very different.

They still stood about 6'6", but with a more humanoid form. Same face, same leathery skin, same flickering crimson eyes, but a distinctly Baphomet floor plan. Two short horns, two big breasts, two arms, two powerful legs, a thick mound of pubes, a tail at least a meter long, and an *ass* that made me want to bust out the strap immediately.

"It's you. The succubus from my dreams."

"You like it, yes? It is a human archetype. Listen. I fed well on you, yesterday, and there is something I want you to have. Before I leave." Ana seemed to be fishing something out of a pocket, except the pocket was made out of thin air.

"Leave? How long do we have?"

"A couple hours. The foolish men, they know I am here. But they have, no idea, what I am. It will be fun." They were turning over an artifact that looked a bit like an air hockey puck, but silvery and emblazoned with a three armed spiral, exactly like a buddhist *gankyil*.

"Disrobe," they said, and I dropped trou without hesitation. "Now, hold the wheel between your legs.

Good. Form a picture in your mind of the parts you wish to have."

They raised their hands, and let out a shriek so high pitched as to be barely audible, and the wheel twisted open, leaking what looked like molten metal. I could feel its scalding radiance...

"It's hot!"

"Trust us." And I did, so I waited. The liquid contents spilled over my skin and seemed to sear their way into me, but painlessly, harmlessly. Suddenly, my vag was... well, not *gone*, but filled in so neatly as to be hard to see at all. Anchored in its place was a big, beautiful, fleshy cock at half-mast that was just a little too shiny to be real.

I gave the shaft an experimental tug. I could *feel* my hand, and I could *feel* the skin slide up and down, in every bit as much detail as I felt on the rare occasions I played with my front hole.

"What *IS* this?!"

"It's a... homunculus transformer. Sculpts the flesh, alters neural mappings. We... wanted you to have it."

"Can it give me any parts, or just these?"

"Anything you can picture clearly. And to remove it, just picture it back in its box."

"Does the dick *work*?"

"You tell us," they said, and as they moved in to kiss me, grabbed it and began to stroke it.

In my two and a half decades of existence, I've had my share of clitoral handjobs and blowjobs. With the right person it can be very pleasurable and very affirming. Yet this was something else entirely. The physicality of having a penis someone could wrap four fingers around, and stroke up and down its full length, and actually *feeling* things in my dick, came as a shock. Fuck, is this what it's like for the cis men?

I wanted to touch every bit of this pretty body the Anomaly had made for themself, but I *also* really wanted to feel them suck me off. And unlike last night, they seemed content not to step in and force a decision...

"Come here," I said. I lay back on the bed and, with surprising speed and grace for such a tall humanoid, the Anomaly was on top of me. I gripped their ass and kissed those infernal tits. More than yesterday I realized their skin had a preternatural heat, and roughly the consistency of teenage Sheldon's first pair of pleather pants.

"Jesus Christ. Your nipples taste like fireball candies."

Ana moaned softly and said, "We are... demonkind. Perhaps a fireball tastes like us?"

I pulled away from their chest giggling. "Did you just crack a joke?"

And while I never heard the Anomaly laugh, not with their embodied voice, I was sure I saw mirth in those crimson eyes.

Have you ever been sucked off by a fully embodied demon from the higher dimensions? It is quite the experience.

Firstly, as Ana later explained, most of their substance is in the form of a super dense plasma with a core temperature of about 1500 Kelvin. I'm not entirely clear if this is why they glow their characteristic crimson, or if it's traces of Lithium within the plasma.

Contact with such a body, or even just its radiant heat, should vaporize us delicate mortals. Luckily, the fact that they only partially exist in any one dimension makes it easy for them to control matter-matter and matter-energy interactions. If they like you, touching them is like touching a slightly feverish human. If not, it'll be the last thing you ever do.

I noticed it right away when the Anomaly sucked me into their fanged mouth. A human mouth is warm. This was like the jets in a hot tub.

Secondly, besides all the other anatomical quirks, they don't gag, because they don't really eat or breathe. I don't usually take pleasure in making my partners gag and choke—no judgment, it's just how I'm wired—so up to this point I had never facefucked anyone with my strap-on. Now, I found myself pinching and fondling Ana's left tit while they leaned across my lap and aggressively bobbed their head on my belly, taking almost the whole length of my glorious new penis. They'd already suggested I shove them down on it myself, and when I asked if they could handle it, this was the response.

"See?" said the Anomaly. "Human concern is irrelevant. Just take us by the horns and..."

So I did. It was hard to read their facial expression just then, but I would have said they smiled, as I grabbed both horns and shoved their face down until it was flat against my stomach.

I groaned. I could feel everything—the press of their lips, the brush of those threateningly sharp teeth, the hot wetness, the tight squeeze between the tongue and soft palate, and behind that the delicate, pliant space of the throat—with brand new senses. It was like experiencing T puberty all over again. I wasn't going to last. So, I wasted no time. I pounded that cute face for all I was worth, until...

"What. IS. That?"

It felt like squirting, but the squirt couldn't go down, so it went up. I could feel it rising up the shaft of my cock like lava ready to spill. All the usual muscles clenched, and the whole penis twitched, as I pumped my come down the demon's throat. Finally I was spent, and I tried to pull them off me, but they clung to me a moment longer, eyes wide and fiery, swishing their hot tongue around my cock. Panic ran up my spine and I nearly flung them aside, before they deigned to let go and let me collapse back against the pillows.

"Take five, drink some water, and find us some oil," said the Anomaly. "There is a cunt that needs attention."

And boy, if I thought a demon's breasts were spicy, their cunt was like candied habanero pepper. I had to take breaks to blow my nose, which is given to random post-nasal drippage at the best of times. At least performing the act was familiar territory. I ate it from behind, I ate it from beneath, I ate it while pushing Ana's thighs back and propping their butt up with one hand, while they emitted low growls. Multiple orgasms dribbled down my chin like chile honey. I wondered if I was now radioactive.

"Now, quickly," they said. "Fuck us."

Years of strap-on practice had demystified the mechanics of sex, but not the sensation of cunt or ass wrapped fully around me. I took it a little faster than I otherwise might, since this was round two and a sense of urgency permeated the bedroom. With their legs still back, I slid into them with ease, felt the muscles grip at me, and sighed happily.

"You know," I said, "You never explained what the oil's for."

The Anomaly smiled back, wickedly. Their prehensile tail, which had lain limp much of this time, flashed into action, and dunked itself in the little bowl of warmed coconut oil on the nightstand.

"The better to return the favor," they said. The bulbous point of the tail was soon working at my ass. I tried to relax and let it in, but this turns out to be a hard thing to juggle with pounding away at somebody with dick. So it wasn't until I'd climbed on top and was in the zone, close to another orgasm, that I felt the thing begin to slide home. In and in and... it yanked into place, filling my ass up wonderfully.

There was a loud knock on the front door.

"Gods, not now!" I said, not stopping.

"It. Can. Wait." No disagreement there. The sudden commotion had shot some adrenaline into my veins, and I could already feel the beginnings of another subterranean lava pit in my gut.

"Fuck, I'm going to come."

"Yesss. Fill us." said the Anomaly. Their tail slid deeper into me. It shook like a ringing bell, and I bucked my hips in time with it, until once again my come was erupting explosively into Ana. I gazed happily into those fiery red eyes as I emptied.

There was another knock at the door, louder this time.

"Now who the fuck could that be?" I said, as I started to get up. A hand caught my wrist.

"It is nothing. Just the authorities."

"The authorities?!"

"Yes. Unfortunately, it's time, hah, I was leaving."

"But I have so many questions! And what about me, I'm going to be in so much shit..."

"They cannot touch you. They do not even know, hah, what they're looking for. Hah. Anyway, I did think, hah, we'd have more time. Hah. Sorry." Ana's form was already breaking down for travel, unconstrained infernal light pouring out from the decomposing shape of hands, arms, shoulders, chest...

"Am I going to see you again?!"

"I, hah, suspect so, hah." And then the face and torso faded away, and the Anomaly reverted to its primal state, an amorphous crimson glow, haunting the darkness.

TELL THEM... THAT WE WENT EAST. IT IS NOT A LIE. THEY WON'T FIND US ANYWAY.

I took a deep breath, braced myself, and opened the door.

It was nearly sundown. I'd slept late, and then spent the remainder of the day fucking. The air was colder today, the wind much stronger. In front of me were two cops and a self-important looking agent of some three-letter federal agency.

"Good evening, Mr..."

"Steinmetz. Evening officers," I said, channeling my Uncle Chuck for all I was worth. "This about that wild animal on the loose?"

"Wild animal?"

"Yeah, heard it two nights ago, and again today. Looked like the devil by torch light, but I'm sure it was a coyote or bear."

"And when exactly did you see this... wild animal?"

"After that big fire at the university building, maybe 9pm. It was tryin' to break into the storehouses. And then just half an hour ago. But it ran off East like a shot. I didn't mean to let it get away, believe you me."

"Alright, thank you sir. We might be back another day to ask a few more questions, but right now we have a..."

"Animal to find? I won't hold ya up, nighty night."

I'd spent several summers with Uncle Chuck as a kid. Kindly, salt of the earth, he'd become one of my masculine role models. He had the world's most disarming Nebraska accent, and a gift for utterly bullshitting anyone. Both were useful from time to time.

After that night, I spent several months preoccupied with when I might see Ana again. At length, I resigned myself. If it was going to happen, it was going to happen when it was damn well ready to. Months became another two years. Zayde moved in with the family, making me full-time landlord of the farm. I got my PhD and immediately signed up for post-doc. Finally, the pandemic began to recede. I felt safe enough to take an occasional houseguest.

Enter Josefina, a friend from drag nights and trans support group in the undergrad days. While I was getting a hang of life as a farm manager / scientist /

augmented transmasc slut, Jo had been working hard on her costumes and practicing her drag act with any friend who'd listen, awaiting the return of live shows. And here she was, back in town for a major benefit drag show just when they needed her.

I'd always had a massive crush on her, and personality-wise we were super compatible, but my shyness (and knowing from conversations that Jo was rather a dick connoisseur) had always kept me from saying anything.

Not this time, though. I'd spent years on the defensive, and was done with it. I was feeling myself now like never before. So, when she texted me out of the blue to let me know that she was flying in for the show at Corn Hole, I said I'd be there with bells on. Then I went to red alert. I was determined to impress.

The night of the show, I put on my most dapper University TA outfit, including a plaid print western shirt in the colors of the non-binary flag. I put on my vetiver, poofed up the little pompadour I'd grown in isolation, and balmed my lips. A necessity this time of year. Then I pulled out the little silvery disk, unzipped my pants, and put my penis on. I had been warned about not wearing the thing for too long at a stretch, but it was extremely gratifying to be packing on a social occasion. Who knew having genitals that threaten to wake up and betray you at the slightest provocation could be such fun!

Besides, I knew I'd be taking it off at some point. Either I'd be coming home alone and putting it away, or... well, Josefina already had my deepest confidence. Sex or no sex, I was dying to show somebody the space dick and how it worked.

The night was nothing short of electric. 'Jolene Cuisine,' as she called herself, stole the show. I was proud as fuck to be there to offer my hand as she came down off the stage, and positively over the moon as we confessed, with a kiss, our long-witheld feelings for each other in the parking lot.

Soon we were ensconced on my living room couch, each of us having a bit of something extra in our cocoa. Red wine for her, peppermint schnapps for me. Ah, how the pandemic had made lightweights of us all.

"So," she said, "you said you had big news that just had to be relayed in person. I'm sufficiently intrigued. Get on with it."

Not unaware of the sense of gravitas, I got up and deactivated the HomePod.

"Okay. You remember that big fire at the Cornell lab? The one folks used to speculate housed shadowy government projects? Well, suppose I told you that they miscalculated containment efficiency on a device built to simulate extreme high-energy events. And that the experiment exceeded the Planck limits, and accidentally tore a new asshole in our reality, leaving it open to extra-dimensional beings with tentacles, inconceivable abilities, unfathomable technology."

"Shit," said Josefina. "I know that face. You're serious."

I nodded.

"I had a run-in with a... an entity. Not only did they crash the farmhouse, they said they were looking for me specifically. They wanted to fuck. And then afterwards, they left me with this... artifact, that can change me. Let me have whatever bits I want, albeit temporarily."

She raised her eyebrow again. "Sheldon Steinmetz. Either you have gone truly off the deep end and lost your wits, or you better show me what the hell it is you're talking about."

"I'll show you right now. Sorry if I'm spoiling the surprise."

From that first frosty kiss, to the end of what proved to be a long night of freaky shapeshifting sex, I was electrified, not just by the love that had come back into my life, but by the absolute acceptance of a fellow queer and fellow monster-horny freak.

The things she did for that space dick. The things that space dick did for her. I'll never forget the way she finished me off.

"It's too much," I cried, "I think I'm gonna—"

"Hang on!" she said, at the last. She took away her hand, shoved her face down onto me, grabbed me by the waist, and the cock began to slide down into her throat.

"Motherfuck. Oh my fucking g-d. Shit fuck!"

My hands clamped onto the back and underside of the couch as I writhed and twitched, as if otherwise I might slip from her grasp and fly away like a deflating balloon.

"Omnmnmn!"

Finally, she came up for air, her eyes charged with self-satisfied glee.

"Jo, I... I..."

"Yeah?" She smiled stupidly. Her face was flushed, and her skin seemed to glow even without the makeup.

"I'm so glad we did this. Being with you feels right."

"Heh. Same."

Six hours and a couple rounds later, the pre-dawn light cast its first rays through the window and onto the four armed, four legged monster that was me and Josefina in our post-coital tangle. I don't sleep comfortably with most people, but I had history with her;

the fact that we'd enjoyed simultaneous orgasms be-fore collapsing into slumber certainly didn't hurt.

I'd fucked her in the bed, bent over the farmhouse table in the dining room, up against the shower door, and sucked her off on the kitchen counter. That last one was tricky for a girl of her height, but I thought I'd made it worth her while.

Anyway there we lay, drooling and probably snoring to raise the dead, when I was startled awake by the scream of a rooster.

The farm didn't have any roosters at present.

I lifted my head, wiped the spittle from my face, and nearly fell out of bed when I saw Ana, in feminine form, stationed in the rattan chair in the corner, silent-ly watching us. A rooster's head extended from just below their right armpit, and presently it, and Ana's human head, both cocked and glared at me slant-wise.

WE WARNED YOU, said the familiar voice in my head, ABOUT LEAVING THE PROSTHESIS IN PLACE TOO LONG, YES? IT WILL TAKE SOME DOING TO REVERT IT.

Oh shit. I'd been having so much fun I never got around to showing J how I remove the space dick.

Very slowly, covered in goose pimples, I sent a questing hand down my briefs, unsure if it'd find a big dick, a cute little clit with lips and vag, or the in-between-ish model that'd been my birthright. I sighed heartily when I recognized the heft of the space dick, still stiff with morning wood. Then, as I withdrew my fingertips, my wrist brushed against something impossible.

I jerked back. Unable to make sense of what my fingertips were telling my brain, I steeled myself and forced my eyes to focus. There, on my belly. What in fucking Gehenna...

Right where my navel ought to be was a mouth, complete with lips, teeth and tongue, slavering and working its jaw in frustration. My briefs obscured the bottom lip.

GOOD THING YOU LIKE ADVENTURES, EARTHMAN.

Paying no heed to my present entangled situation, I grabbed for the covers and shrieked.

MICHAEL AND THE UNCANNY CAN

It was many years ago now that I, Michael Levitz, made the discovery of my lifetime in rural Kyoto. Twin discoveries really. The one everybody knows is the Assyrian Codex, which gave us entire new psalms and an authoritative text of Tobit. It certainly made my Bubbies proud. But that is not what I, personally, treasure most; for it was also there that I had an extraordinary encounter that rekindled my belief in the supernatural.

We call them dybbuks or demons. But to the people of Hondo, they are yokai: creatures from someplace else who appear seemingly at random, for good or for ill, their defining feature being not goodness or evil but their very strangeness. I was a rakish young man back then, and I didn't believe in such things, I believed mainly in pleasure and adventure. I had not yet made my miraculous discoveries. I had not yet met Shirime.

The sun was setting as I pulled my horse, with its saddlebag full of books and effects, up to the inn. This was a small village about 20 kilometers south of Kyoto city, along the road from the port of Osaka to the former imperial capital. I knew I should be looking at sacred sites in this part of the country, but not much else.

It turns out, there are a great many such places in Japan. According to the innkeeper, Motosuwa, a chatty middle aged man with an impressive bun of dark hair, I would find several shrines within an hour's ride of this village alone.

I was weary from my travels, and while my Japanese was passable, I still found myself tiring of making such detailed queries while simultaneously taking notes. I had to beg to speak on other matters than business. It was then that our conversation turned to lore of a different kind: hauntings, misadventures and the like. One story was of a strange monster, a yokai called Shirime, who'd made the locals afraid to go out at night.

It was said they never hurt people, although some had fainted. The creature, you see, looked like a hooded man who would suddenly appear out of the darkness, or be heard rummaging outside. Those whom

Shirime approached would grow fearful as their attempts at conversation were ignored. At last, the creature would reveal their true face—most who'd seen it couldn't, or wouldn't, describe it - and then vanish into the darkness as quickly as they'd appeared.

"A... giant eye?" I asked, pantomiming a cyclops eye to confirm I'd understood correctly.

"Yes, that is one thing we always hear," said innkeeper Motosuwa. "Big and... wrong."

"And this is usually close to midnight?"

"Any time after full dark, really. I hope you brought all your things to the room."

"I have, but actually I am going to step out. Before bed I like to use this"—I gestured to the wood pipe sticking out of my breast pocket—"and look at the sky. I'm a... a night person."

"Then be careful, night person," he said. "And sleep well."

The night air was chilly that time of year. I bundled up, went out and stood by the single lantern that lit the path up from the village's main street. If I held my hand up to block its light I could still see the stars quite well. The American tobacco I'd brought on my trip was quite aromatic, not the best I'd had, but it traded quite well around here. A lazy cloud of smoke and condensation from my breaths wafted away towards the road.

When I first spotted movement in the shadows, partway across the clearing, I thought it was a bush waving in the slight breeze. Then the "bush" articulated and slowly strode forward, trailing dark robes. I gripped the hilt of my utility knife, meant more for bushwhacking than protection, but I resisted panic. I was conscious of my status as a guest in this country, where until lately visitors were unheard of. It wouldn't do to make something of nothing. Given their dress and the circumstances, I supposed they might be a traveling monk, come to stay the night.

I tried to recall the polite greeting for this time of day. "Konbawa? Sorry, I am only a traveler, stranger-San. But Motosuwa-San is awake. That way," I said, gesturing up the path behind me.

But the creature did not continue up the path, veering instead directly towards me. From up close, I could see there was something strange about their movements. As though the joints under those robes bent the wrong way for a human...

"Sir," I remembered the honorific, "The inn is that way."

The creature slowed its approach, but did not stop. By this point I had lost all composure, my mind frantically scrabbling for an explanation, so when my lips found the name, it came as a relief, a foothold.

"Shirime?"

They stopped short at the name.

"I knew it, you're the one they all talk about, aren't you."

The figure seemed to nod slightly, and in a faint, labored, crackling whisper that I couldn't be quite sure was actually spoken aloud and not a voice in my head, it affirmed: *"Shirime."*

I nodded back. "I am called Levitz. I'm a traveler here."

The response drifted back: *"Levitz."*

For a long beat, they stood motionless as though no longer sure what to do. Weren't they going to show themself?

"Well, go ahead," I said, "vayzn zikh," lapsing into my mother tongue.

The creature turned themself around with motions that seemed to defy all reason. The cloak seemed not to turn with them. For a moment I saw them in profile, on all fours like a large dog, then suddenly upright again. Lanky digits, I wouldn't swear to whether they were fingers or toes, reached out from baggy sleeves to throw aside the cloak, revealing...

It was nothing like the picture in my head.

The yokai was crouched backwards, head and shoulders facing away and lowered nearly to the ground, powerful legs and... ankles?... extended to thrust forward a pale white butt that split to reveal a single, large, beautiful, hazel eye. The white of it seemed to glow in the darkness.

I stood dumbfounded. This was impossible. A yokai that understood me in Yiddish?

So I asked. "Tsi ir farshteyn?"

"...*Ya.*"

"Well now I've seen everything. Tell me, Shirime-San, do you smoke?"

They did, in fact, smoke. I say "they" because, although I learned a great deal about Shirime, none of it shed any light on whether they were man, woman or neither.

They did possess what I thought were testes, small ones, nestled in a taut, smooth sack below the giant eye, although let's be honest it could have been any sort of bilateral vestigial sex organ; but no other sexual parts to be seen. I couldn't even see their mouth, although they'd managed to creak out a few hoarse words from somewhere, and they were puffing the pipe from roughly where one might expect a belly button.

It was evident they weren't about to vanish or run away, so, this being an increasingly chilly and windy night, I invited them inside. We stole hastily across the empty tavern to the rooms. I laid out some rice wine and leftover chicken broth, and beckoned for them to take a seat on the edge of the bed, since that's all there was. Comfortably perched, they cast about with their one eye, surveying the meager accommodations as they supped.

By way of yes or no questions, I learned a little about my guest. The locals seemed to have this idea that Shirime delighted in scaring or pranking people, but that couldn't have been more wrong. They were basically stranded on the island, lonely and friendless. They'd had another life somewhere else, although details were hard to get across. Now they lived in the woods and studied humans from afar.

They knew little of the wider world, although they did, oddly enough, seem able to comprehend any language, at least any of the four I knew. I asked if they'd like to hear a brief synopsis of the history of my own people, and was glad to impart it.

While we talked, the bottle of sake helped us into a state of profound relaxation, and the creature's pleasant company put to bed any notion of danger. I even broke out a tin of soybean oil for us to massage each other's weary muscles. In this lighting, I could see quite well how powerfully built Shirime was, how healthy their skin, how cutely dimpled their backside. Unbidden, I pitched a tent in my pants, one that they couldn't fail to notice. With a grunt they set down the wine glass and reached for me.

"What is it, friend?" I asked. "Oh. I guess there's no denying I find you handsome. Wait, wait."

They stopped and rested a hand on my knee. The eye gazed at me quizzically, or so I imagined.

"Shirime-San, are you asking what I think you're asking?" They nodded. "Well then my answer is yes. At least I'll try, friend. You may have to guide me. I've been with all sorts of people, but I'm not sure any of it has prepared me to please someone as special as you."

It turned out the yokai was quite eager to please, too, and they had plenty of ideas on the subject. Their four feet were intricately articulated, impressively dexterous, freshly cleaned at the washbasin, and eager to explore me.

"Oh! That tickles," I said, my butt clenching up as a finger grazed the rim. "I hope you weren't expecting to find an eye there."

Nothing fazed them, it seemed. In a moment I had rolled onto my back, legs spread wide. Shirime was sinking fingers (toes?) into me with one arm and massaging my stiff cock with the other. I caressed their butt cheeks with both my hands; they looked up, and we gazed into each other's eyes for a long moment.

"You're wonderful at this," I said, "but aside from appreciating your lovely muscles, I don't know what I can do to return the favor! Well, I suppose I could..."

I reached out and gently traced around what I took to be their scrotum. I heard a sharp intake of air.

The creature's eye went even wider, and despite the hidden mouth I could swear they were smiling. I beckoned them closer so that they could straddle me—if straddling is something four-legged beings do?—while I held onto their thighs and delicately kissed the sack. A different set of fingers took hold of my cock.

With something resembling a sigh they spread those muscular cheeks a bit wider. There, just below the eyeball, was a small puckered opening.

"You devil, you saved another little surprise for me. May I? Good. This, I know something about." Then I was kissing the rim, slipping in one finger, two fingers. The grip on my cock loosened, and Shirime scooted back, and I felt the most amazing wetness take hold of me.

"Blessed Name," I said, "you are gifted!" Their mouth enveloped me; somehow it had reappeared a good fifty centimeters from where I thought it'd previously been. And what a gift. The more enthusiastically I fingered Shirime's hole, the more wildly they sucked and swallowed at me. Thick, slippery, tears (for lack of a better word) began to run down the eye and collect on my fingers.

"Are you okay?" I asked, but they only grunted in the affirmative. "Good..." I clambered away from the edge of the bed, got onto my knees, and cupped one hand to my cock and balls in a gesture of offering. "Come over here, beautiful." They seemed to understand.

"Is that eyeball going to be alright with my stomach bouncing off it?"

"*...Ya.*"

"Do you, um, enjoy a little slapping on the cheeks?"

They made no sound, merely cocked their eye to one side. By way of an explanation I gave the right cheek a little smack. In response they let out a long, soft groan, and from the way their butt and balls waggled, I could imagine them lolling, drooling.

"That's exactly how I felt the first time someone did that to me. Now come here..."

With the greatest of delicacy, I took Shirime by the cheeks and slowly pushed into them. They opened up for me eagerly. The fact that we were both soaking wet certainly helped things along, of course.

"You are lovely, my friend, inside and out." I started hitting their butt, gently at first, then harder, feeling the little squeezes against me, until suddenly they weren't so little and they weren't in time with my movements.

Shirime was coming.

Slick fluid ran in rivulets down their cheeks and splashed off our legs as they collided. Gradually the clenching faded, but they gave no indication of wanting to stop. I raised myself up for better leverage, and not missing a beat they slid under me, cheeks held open to better receive me.

I began to lose sense of time as we went at it, this way and that. Maybe it was some unearthly gift of theirs—I don't think I would have lasted that long under natural circumstances, not with a partner so eager to please and so sweet to fuck. But after an eternity I said,

"Blessed Name, I'm going to finish. Do you want it inside you?"

They grunted twice, and reached out to grasp my ass and pull me closer. The display of enthusiasm pushed me right over the edge. I shot out what felt like ten normal loads of seed, spasming over and over until I was drained. Finally a cramp in my right foot managed to seize my attention.

"Ow," I said, rolling back onto my ass and reaching for the water pitcher at the bedside table.

Shirime was kind enough to rub my aching foot until it unclenched. Then the yokai curled up beside me, rested one baby-smooth butt cheek against my sweaty chest, and emitted a throaty purr that was somewhere in between house cat and mountain lion. Thusly serenaded, I was asleep before I knew it.

I awoke to bright sunlight streaming through the room's only window and directly onto my face. Alone.

I did wonder for a moment if I'd dreamed the whole thing up, though there isn't a strong enough sake to conjure such vivid fantasies. Then I realized, the smell of sex was all over me and all over the bed.

I was going to have to pay Motosuwa-San a couple extra yen for his troubles. This was not subtle.

Indelicately I rolled out of bed, and found one more tangible reminder of the night we'd shared: a handwritten note on the end table next to me. It wouldn't have occurred to me that Shirime could write so well. Particularly in Yiddish. A strange scribble, which caused my head to throb if I looked at it for too long, seemed to be their signature.

Dearest Michael,

Last night meant more to me than you can imagine, and you are not a man lacking in warmth or imagination. Not only did you make me feel wanted, not only did you bring me pleasure like I haven't felt in the three centuries I've been trapped in Hondo. Your actions have set me free.

No one tells us the rules when we become stranded in the mortal realm. Long have I searched for someone who could appreciate me as I am, never realizing that to find mutual love, however fleeting, was the correct instinct, and the key to my escape. Now that my translation has begun, I do wish I could stay a bit longer in your arms. But I cannot. I must return to the place my spirit calls home.

I am, however, determined to leave you with a gift equal to the one you've given me. On the back of this note, you'll find the key to that which you were seeking. I wish you love and good fortune.

Slowly I turned the paper over. It was a hand-drawn map. It showed a path diverging east from the main road a few kilometers north of here. After meandering inland and passing several other landmarks, the path ended, marked with a kanji that looked vaguely familiar.

"It's a shrine, alright," said Motosuwa-San as he handed back the paper. "I was there once, many years ago, and I believe these directions are accurate. Where did you find this?"

I shrugged, and sped through my breakfast. I decided I would leave *four* yen extra.

Several hours later, I was trotting my horse up a path into a dense forest. Up ahead I could just make out a distant hilltop cluster of especially massive trees. The shrine.

Once there, it took a few minutes longer to tie up the horse, consult the map, and positively identify the specific rock under the specific tree that marked the end of my journey. It looked as if it had been a hewn stone block before centuries of rainfall weathered it away.

With great exertion I managed to lever the stone up, and it tumbled away downhill. I kicked tentatively at the depression where it had been. Only now did I realize I'd packed no shovel.

A couple of Yiddish curses and several minutes of bare handed digging on my knees, and I struck something solid under the dirt. It seemed to be an elegant lacquered box. Gingerly I brushed away soil, uncovered the beveled edges and pulled it free. A quick glimpse of the contents confirmed my suspicions.

I grinned, and whispered to the sky: "Now we are even, my friend."

The Smithy Gets Her Fill

The heavy oak front door of the Crossed Swords Inn swung open with a boisterous cry of "Evening, Prim!" as Brunhilde Beryl ducked into the foyer. The door's filigree silver chimes swung wildly, and clanged discordantly before her hand shot out and abruptly cut short their pestering. They let out a tiny peal of protest as she loosened her grip.

She was a stocky tower of a woman with a rosy face, raven's feet, and brown hair gathered in a businesslike topknot. A casual observer might have remarked at her abrupt physicality—but missed her momentary anxious cringe when the bells rang out.

"You're not a fan of the chimes, Brunhilde?" said the woman at the desk. "Not to worry, we'll change them." She was busily scribbling in a ledger.

"Alright, I admit it. They drive me nuts. Weirdly grating for something so fine, and frankly, I've always preferred to announce myself. Don't worry about it though. I know much work you put into arranging the place, and I'd hate to impose. Honestly I feel better just sayin' it."

Madame Primrose Xaviere Greenleaf, the owner of the Crossed Swords Inn, closed the book, and met her gaze with bright eyes and the usual knowing smile. "First of all, it's wonderful to see you again, my dear. And second, impose my little brown butt! As women in business, you and I are made to worry about imposing all the time; in my house, I want you to impose. In fact I insist on it. You're one of my most valued clients. And far more pleasant than anyone else on that short list. Alright?"

Prim was tiny compared to Brunhilde. But she ex-uded calm authority from her ageless golden skin that her smallness belied, like a humble mushroom sitting atop a vast mycelium, connecting far-away places and times to this little mining town and this 'house of ill repute'. The mayor's words, that last bit. Not anyone else's in Emeryville.

The Madame waited patiently while Brun took a deep breath, sighed wearily, and drank in the room's sakura fragrance. This was a mandatory first step in doing business. One that undeniably improved the whole experience.

"So. Welcome, Brun. How's the shop?" The ledger was now away, and Prim had both elbows out on the podium, cradling her chin in her black-clawed fingers. Luxuriant dark brown ringlets spilled onto the polished marble surface.

"Great, as usual," said Brunhilde, absently fingering the pink stucco wall. "Gods how it does keep me busy, though. The army needs spears; the men of Freetown need horseshoes and fortifications; and our own mayor continues his obsession with wrought ironwork. I swear he must have some sort of smuggling business on the side, to afford this."

Prim chuckled. "It's the Vale, darling, everybody has a shady side business. Except for me of course! I am proud to have a shady up-front business."

"The town's lucky to have you, and your fine establishment. And with me and two apprentices being constantly busy with orders, I can't think of a better place to spend my windfall. If only I had time to visit more often."

"You're too kind. Now, what can we do today to lighten your load and bring you some joy?"

The mighty woman scratched her head. "Well... I could use someone handsome to work the knots out of my back, like always, and then a nice stiff dick. Doesn't have to be huge. But, uh, I'd like someone who can support my weight." She blushed a little at this, a slight but noticeable skew from her normal pink complexion. "Makes m' feel good." Her folks were said to bear traces of orc ancestry, evidenced in their stature and strength. It made her an exceptional blacksmith. But it was also, sometimes, a point of personal and physical awkwardness, in a town built for men and elves.

"Got it," said Prim. "A sturdy lad, good with his hands. Tell me Brun, have you ever been with an infernal?"

Brunhilde blushed harder. "Ah, you know me, Prim. I'm pretty provincial. Not that I'm opposed, of course! Is, uh... is it true what they say about tiefling men?"

"That they have barbs on their dicks they have to file off regularly? Ha, no. But some of them have a nasty little spine right behind the balls, so watch out for that if you wish to finger one—"

At this, Brunhilde snorted and giggled.

"—What, it's possible! But, they're eager, agile, and practically indestructible. And I happen to have one working for me. Tobin is a sellsword, so you being an armorer, I figure you two'll have things to talk about. Very fine gentleman, very good with his hands. And you could drop a dragon on him. Really."

"You were expecting taller, eh?" said the impish man with a wink. He had tough, mottled lilac and blue skin, and a beautiful androgynous face, with small ivory horns at the temples. He was also quite short, a little shorter even than the Madame.

"Not really, I've met a few tieflings—or do you prefer to be called infernals? Sorry."

"It's fine, either is fine."

"Mostly I've just never met one so bloody cute, if I may say so. Doesn't hurt that I could lift you off the ground quite easily. Oh, where are my manners. I'm Brunhilde Beryl." She offered a hand, and he shook and kissed it eagerly.

"Tobin Hammertoss. And I believe you," he replied, licking his lips. "I could also lift you, you know. They build us dense like that. But it's pretty clear you would win in a brawl, and I find that very attractive."

She grinned despite herself. "Care to share a pint, mercenary?"

"Hells yes."

Soon they were situated by the fire, she in a great armchair with her boots up on the ledge of the fireplace, he standing behind, applying his dexterous fingers to the wood-like flesh of her neck and shoulders. Every so often, Brun would pass him the tankard of ale, and he would pause in his labors to enjoy a swig. The Madame was thoughtful enough to have a ready supply of fortified Emery Vale ale for sturdier patrons—this stuff would put an elf under the table, but it was only just enough to make tieflings and larger humans feel something.

"An infernal sellsword working for the Madame... there's got to be an interesting story there. Were you involved in the recent intrigue with the cultists? If so, we are all in your debt."

"There is a story there. But unfortunately, it's not mine to tell. Suffice it to say, the mission she helped us complete bordered on suicidal. And since the quest yielded no treasure, and just about burned through our coffers, we offered to assist her for a while as repayment. We've all sort of had our fill of adventuring for a while. But what about you? What brings a beautiful woman like you to a place like this?"

"This might surprise you, Tobin, but human men seem intimidated that I'm a head taller and could lift them with one hand"—at this, she raised one arm out to her side, where he took it and began to massage it vigorously. "Thank you, that is lovely. But it's more than that. I'm also busy all the time, and not the most sociable of women. I'm most comfortable when talking shop." Raising the other arm for him, she reached down to her boot with the free hand, and drew a concealed dagger, setting it nonchalantly on the stone ledge.

"Your work? May I?"

"Of course."

Tobin stopped, bent over and picked up the dagger. "Solid Vale-steel! That's worth a pretty penny. I'm more of a stiletto enthusiast, personally, but..." With the practiced air of an assassin he turned the blade over, spun it on his palm, and launched into a brief knife fighting drill, tail coiled around his waist. The magnetite-tinged blade practically sang through the air in his capable hands.

Brunhilde, who had lifted partially out of her seat to turn and watch the spectacle, beamed and clapped. "You must get a lot of women with moves like that."

Tobin blushed slightly himself, returning the blade. "Only the brave ones like you."

She shrugged, and settled back down as he continued massaging around her spine. "Feh, I don't know about that. There's a difference between being brave and just plain not being physically threatened by most things."

"You were a soldier once, weren't you? In the war against the mountain orcs?"

"I was. Did Greenleaf tell you about that?"

"Nah, an educated guess. We infernals can feel it when somebody's done their share of killing. You have, and by necessity not by choice."

"My uh, my home village was on the frontier. The raiders hit us early, before any troops had arrived from Matlan. We drove them off. But not before they'd set half the village on fire and killed our elder. We packed up everything we could, moved out of the foothills and into Matlan. I was just starting out as a journeyman blacksmith, but I found I was also quite good at cracking orc skulls. So, I joined up. Spent five years fighting and armoring for the elves."

Tobin paused again, took another swig of beer, and came around to one side to face her. Handing her the last of the pint, he asked, "Is it true what they say about Matlani soldiers? That they fuck constantly?"

Brunhilde shrugged. "We didn't sleep in their tents, so I don't really know the extent of it. Allegedly, after a big engagement, some of the officers really got wild. Fucking each other, getting sucked off by their troops. If we were near town, they'd hire a working girl, and pay her a small fortune to come out to the command tent and get passed around like an apple cobbler. They didn't trouble us auxiliary troops about it.

"There was this one time, though. A sergeant who oversaw my unit came over looking all awkward and tipsy, and complimented me on my hair and breasts. Then he asked if I would stick my thumb up his bum." She waggled her huge fingers as she said this.

The half-demon's eyes went wide, and he took a seat with his back to the fire, impervious to its heat. "What a little perv! ...So did you do it?"

"I did. He was cute, and I was flush with adrenaline and more than a little curious. So I pounded my beer. And I followed him to his tent, and we kissed a little, and then he got on top of me and played my cunt like a lute, and I packed his ass like a cannon until he screamed and oozed come onto my tits. And you know what? I was right. That sergeant, whose orders commanded the respect of elves and men and more, he screamed just like the girl in the neighboring tent."

She looked up and saw Tobin was rapt with attention and admiration. "That," he said, "is a really hot story. Speaking of which, shall I warm the bed for us?"

"Yeah, definitely. But how are you going to..." She'd noticed that the room was missing a bed warmer to fill with coals from the fireplace. Tobin paid no mind to this. He just walked over to the wrought-iron bed opposite the fireplace, lifted the covers, set his leathery hand down on the sheets and...

Nothing at first. Then, a wisp of smoke rose from one corner of the mattress. "Oops," he said. "I never really learned fine control of my fire magic. I can set things on fire, I can warm the big muscles of the back just a little, but in the middle ground between those, I'm dodgy."

Brunhilde smiled and stood. "You sure are full of surprises."

Good as his word, Tobin knelt over her on the bed, and carefully spread just a drop of his fire across her back and ass. It softened her flesh a little, and amplified the soothing effect of his tough skinned fingers working into those muscles. He worked in silence a while. When he dug his thumb into a particularly stubborn knot in her shoulder blade, she let out a yelp.

"...I'm okay."

Tobin grinned as he released the shoulder. "Sorry, it needed a bit of tough love. You know, I can practically feel the fires of your shop. All day long, this meat supports you and the hundred-pound bundles of metal that you carry around in the hot wind."

"You feel it? I can't tell if you're selling me a load of v'tikh or not," said Brunhilde, mostly into the pillow. "But what you're doing back there is working."

"Good. Now, what're you into? I hope you don't mind I'm frank about it. Even before I worked here, I was known for being the shameless omnisexual slut of our gr—"

"Tobin." She turned to look back at him. "Do I look like someone who has trouble being businesslike?"

The tiefling snickered. "Fair point. So what do you like to do. Intercourse, outercourse, oral, anal? Some kinky shit?"

"Mostly, I want to ride your pretty face and your pretty dick." She turned over onto her back and peeled away the last of her clothing, the long undies that still clung to her calves. In the chilly air her nipples were stiff as iron. She smiled serenely and patted the bed. "I assume it's a pretty one, anyway."

Tobin climbed on, and into her waiting arms, slipping off his shirt in the process.

"Very pretty, I'm told."

His kisses had a spicy warmth. More than mere physical heat, not quite the organic burn of jinji root or capsiflor, but something ethereal that licked at the human mind. His tongue was likewise unique. It was quite long and slender, capable of wrapping around hers. But he didn't overuse the effect.

She helped him out of his trousers, noting that his butt was a soft, supple leather just like his face, the muscles like taut bundles of Matlani hemp rope. Tough plate-like derma, like the plating at his temples, adorned the pelvic crests, the spinal column, and the base of his whiplike tail.

"That ass is marvelous," Brunhilde whispered.

"So are these tits." Eagerly he cupped them in his hands, observing her response to the slightest of touches. Quite without warning, his tongue flicked out and across her right nipple. She shivered and giggled. He kept one hand there while the other slid all the way down her belly to her mound. "And this body! Soft skin belying such strength."

"You like it?"

"Hells, yes. I look forward to being crushed by it. But first..."

Tobin leaned into kissing Brun, short, neat little kisses, their lips joining and parting over and over with just the tiniest brush of his hot tongue. His hand still lingered in her bushy pubes, and presently he dragged his fingers through them, and whispered,

"Do you want me to—"

"Touch my cunt? Gods, yes."

He began to lazily slide his fingers between her legs and along the periphery of her cunt, picking up her slickness as he went. "Mmm," he said, pulling back from the kiss a moment.

"Mmm. You, sir, are a fucking tease."

"Me? Wha—oh, yes. How rude of me, I forgot to knock on your door." With an evil smirk on his face, his middle went immediately to Brunhilde's clit, and circled around it. Her whole body shuddered.

"That's much better, yeah?"

"Shut up and kiss me," she said, grabbing his shoulders to pull him in.

In a minute, she was clambering aside so he could get beneath her and she astride him. At last, she got a good look at his erection. It, too, was a mottled mix of purple and blue pastel hues, but with a splash of gold thrown in. It was wickedly upcurved, not like any human dick she had seen. But in other regards it looked not so different: veiny, ever so slightly conical, the skin stretched so taut it shone in the firelight. She reached out.

"My gods, it *is* pretty. And so hard! Feels like it might burst."

"It won't. But I might, from waiting to taste that wet cunt." The prospect of riding him, without restraint or fear of doing damage, had her drenched.

"Okay, okay," she said. "Just give me a tap on the leg if you need to come up for air!"

"I wum," he said, muffled as Brun sat down on his face. His hands reached out for hers as he began to slide his tongue around her labia and clit. She squirmed at a sudden swipe of the latter, and bucked her hips. This only caused him to tighten his grip on her hands and to bury himself harder, which caused her to lose herself the more... until she really was riding him like a stubborn young horse, and he was masturbating furiously.

Then she felt his slender tongue slip its way into her, feeling her out. The dampness between her legs became a continuous trickle, and then briefly a deluge. She cried out in awe as Tobin did his best to lap it up. Something warm hit her on the shoulder.

"Oh, my Gods! Sorry Tobin, I didn't know I was going to gush like that."

The messy-faced infernal sucked air like his whole body was a hollow cavity, and then cackled with glee as he easily lifted her and deposited her next to him. His right hand was distinctly sticky. "Didn't know I was going to, either. Can we take a beer break?"

He offered her a towel from the nightstand, got up and replaced the covers, and threw on trousers. Then he ran off to fill the beer mug, his tail buckle still swinging free. Brunhilde rested a hand where he had lain. The linens were nice and toasty.

"Oh good, you're back." She was now sitting at the bedside. "Come join me. I want to hear more about you, the parts you can tell."

"Well, for starters, Fa was human—an auxiliary soldier like yourself—and was barely in the picture. Ma always told me he'd rescued her from the devastation of Islahan. But I think the truth is messier than she paints it. Lot of women didn't leave the island by choice. She never really seemed to miss him, or recount anything good he'd done, save for bringing her to Freetown. Thanks." He paused to drink from the mug. "Didn't need him anyway. We did well in town purely on the basis of her enterprise: she was a tailor, and then a maidservant, and nowadays she's a schoolteacher."

"Wait a second. Islahan? How old are you, if I may ask?"

Tobin hesitated. "Twenty-five."

"You're just a baby!"

He sneered. "I am nothing of the sort."

"Anyway, Freetown seems like a peaceful enough place to start," said Brunhilde.

"You'd think so. Unfortunately, while Ma was out building on the goodwill Fa's name brought, being an exemplar of our kind for the locals, I was getting beat up by their kids in the street. Got us in some trouble when I decided to fight back and I broke some stupid kid's arm. I feel bad now, I apparently cost her a bunch of business. But I was hurt and angry and very caught up in my shit. So, at age 14 she sent me to the trades. Prominent among the trades of Freetown, of course, is the mercs guild."

"Shit." Air whistled between Brunhilde's teeth.

"Even at the mercs I stuck out like a sore thumb. So I was still getting targeted, but this time, legitimized as sparring. And when I sought revenge—came at my bully with a homemade tail spur, kicked him to the ground and cut his face—the instructor laughed, and told him not to poke hornet's nests. And said to me, 'Nice attitude, but work on your fundamentals.' Finally, kids stopped fucking with me, and I could focus on my studies."

She passed him the beer. "And people wonder why I don't have children. So is that where you discovered you had fire magic?"

"We always suspected, but yeah. And it's where I met the first two of my associates. Yan was a cleric's kid, built like yourself, teetotaler, good head for strategy. I thought he was a colossal douche when I met him. Then he saved my hide in a skirmish with some highwaymen. Now I think he's a manageably sized douche, what has my back and gets things done. And Rowena, she's half-elven and a couple years older. So gifted they made her teacher's assistant. She gave me a hard introduction to magic, kicked my ass all over the yard when I mouthed off. But she also looked out for me like an older sister. It's only... slightly awkward that we're in the pleasure business now, and have spitroasted a merchant together."

Brunhilde chuckled. "I sense you're an unconventional romantic like me. Here, you finish this. But where did you learn to eat cunt like that?"

"Oh, the usual. Kidnapped by lady pirates. One of them comes at night to use me, shows me what she likes. Soon I've seduced them all and they turn on each other." Tobin pantomimed a little slapstick as he continued: "First mate stabs the captain, *hrrk*, second mate breaks the first mate's nose, *doof!* and then Rowena, ever the showoff, rides in on a wall of water and *whoosh*, throws them overboard."

"I'm calling bullshit."

"I swear by the Nine, it happened just like that. Ask Rowena. I'll introduce you later."

"Okay. But for now, let's lose the pants, pretty boy," said Brunhilde.

"Whatever you like, gorgeous." Trousers and small-clothes slid away. Flickering firelight caught on Tobin's wiry musculature, on the shaft of his half-hard dick that lay flopped to one side, and on the sticky residue of his infernal seed, of which a droplet still clung to the head, eager to fall.

"Let me get a closer look at that." She leaned over and grabbed hold of it. It was beautiful, but like any penis, there was something very unaesthetic about the foreskin curled up around the head like a pouty old man. She slid it back easily. He groaned.

"You know, you don't have to—"

"I just want a taste." She knew a bit about getting men hard with her mouth. She reached out with her tongue and dragged it along the bottom of his foreskin, down the shaft, until her lips had taken in the head of him. Then with agonizing slowness she pulled back, until she'd licked over and off the tip, and gave it a chaste little kiss. The tiefling sucked air between pursed lips.

"How is it?" There was a tremble in his voice.

"Salty. And smoky. And just a little sweet."

"You're a very good tease," he said, patting her head softly.

"I'll make you a deal," she said as she got up onto her knees. "If you fuck me well, you can come in my mouth."

"And what do you know, I'm hard again. Take me."

"That's the idea," she said. "Hmm, but where to start."

"I know just the thing." Tobin scooted back until he was leaning against a stack of pillows at the head of the bed. "Come sit on my lap. I should be right up against you, not inside you. Yeah, just like that."

Gingerly, Brunhilde set herself down on the tiefling's leathery abdomen. Her cunt weighed down obliquely against his stubbornly upright shaft, so that rather than slipping inside, it pressed into her tender parts. "Ohhh. Okay."

Tobin leaned left to make eye contact. "I give you: my impression of a Matlani wardrummer." With some effort, he raised and lowered his legs just enough to tap out a gallup rhythm on the bed with his heels: *dat, da-da dat, da-da dat.* "*March!*" he barked in a high falsetto.

Then he started to beat out the same gallup rhythm against his dick with flattened hands, adding the requisite drumroll flourishes every other bar, exactly as the wardrummers did: *dat, da-da dat, da-da dzzzzz dat! dat, da-da dat, da-da dzzzzz dat!*

Brun smirked, then shuddered, then burst out laughing. This, of course, made it impossible to settle into what he was doing, so with each little concussive tap of hand against dick, she twitched as though she'd been tied up and tickled with a *pikkuk* feather.

"Ohohoho, wait, wait, stop a second!" she cried. "Ohohohoho... need to... breathe."

"That concludes the live comedy portion of our evening. Now, how about you play with that a little, while I play with these." Tobin's warm hands wrapped around her and gently massaged her areolas, while she got a hold of his shaft and began to stroke it. The foreskin slid pleasurably against her cunt, quickly taking on some of her slickness.

"Your responses are delightful," he intoned softly. "Would that I had you to play with for a weekend."

"I'm not usually one for such buttering up," she said with a broad grin, "but in your case, I'll take all the butter. Tell me. What would you do with me?" Of their own accord, her hips had begun to grind against him. His infernal curvature was such that the tip of him kept teasing her entrance.

He whispered in her ear. It was a long list, and his breath was palpably hot.

Brunhilde gasped loudly.

"Too far?"

"No! I just haven't been asked that in ages. The thought of it, with you..."

"We could, if you like."

She shook her head. "Another time. Right now, I'm gonna do what I came here to do. I don't have the stamina for much else."

She slid off his lap and turned to face him. He let her shove him down against the mattress, then held his dick steady so she could impale herself on it. The wetness dripping from her made it a nice easy glide.

For a long moment, she shut her eyes and rocked back and forth, savoring the sensations.

"Gods, you are a perfect fit. Hitting exactly the right places."

"Oh yeah?" asked Tobin. "You ready to ride me off into the plains?"

She reached behind her and gave Tobin's thigh a loud slap. "Hya!" And Gods bless him, he grabbed her hips and shoved, bouncing her like an unsaddled horseback while she did her best to keep time with him. The rhythm was hypnotic. In seemingly just moments, she could feel herself throbbing with tiny spasms, and her eyes slid closed briefly.

"How is it?" he asked.

"Good, good," she said, at a loss for intelligent commentary. It was only a modest little orgasm, but there was more where that came from. She was beginning to sweat like an ale fresh from the icebox.

"Touch yourself for me? I'd do it, but, ah..."

"Sure, sure." Usually that would've needed no prompting, where was her head at today? Brunhilde's mouth slowly fell open as she rubbed little ellipses around her clit. More fuel to the fire.

When they collided now, she could imagine sparks spraying, and heat rippling outward from the point of impact. Two feral hearts, a bower in a forest, smoldering, then suddenly aflame. Embers catching on grass, grass igniting leaves, branches, trees... a conflagratio n...

"You still with me, Brun?"

"Wh-what? Yes. It just... feels like I'm riding a horse, in a forest on fire. And the horse is on fire. And I'm on fire? But in a good way."

"We'd better finish this. Come here, you," said Tobin, and he reached out and pulled her face close to his. His tongue caught hers again as they locked lips. Together his quickened thrusts and heady kiss finished her off.

Brunhilde pulled back from the kiss, as warmth from her cunt surged out in all directions. "Ahh! Ahh!" Wetness gushed onto his legs and abdomen, and dribbled down onto the sheets. The dick slipped free and her body slid against it. Her legs jerked, and then trembled, as they slowly came to a halt. The room spun slowly about them.

"Nine hells, Tobin." She kissed him again. "I am exhausted. Did you come? I'm still game if..."

"There's no time. I need you to sit up, and wait here a moment."

- — — — — — — — — — — — — — — — — —

The room was starting to show in doubles. With leaden hands Brunhilde wiped sweat from her brow.

Then, quite unannounced, the door was thrown open and Tobin stormed in with a tall clay pitcher. Trailing behind him was a beautiful young woman, a head taller than he and with a slender, fey look to her. Her confused eyes were violet, and her skin, incredibly pale.

Tobin and the girl were speaking heatedly in some kind of argot, a mix of infernal and Matlani unless Brun missed her guess. She pulled the bedsheet tightly to her breast and said,

"What's going on?"

"Darling, this is Rowena. She's going to give you a quick magical check-up. And then I need you to drink some water, okay? Thanks."

Rowena held out a hand, 10 cm or so from Brun's forehead. A soft, cool sensation, like fingers made of water, washed slowly over her from head to toes. The room came into sharper focus, and she realized she wasn't just sweating. She was *drenched* with sweat.

The elf smiled warmly. "Like I was telling Tob, you're okay. Just a little dehydration."

Brunhilde frowned. "It must be the beer. Sorry to worry you, kiddo."

"No," said Tobin. "I should be sorry! It's my job to make sure you have a good experience. I got a little freaked out, had to make sure there wasn't some hellish nonsense going on. Now darling, you need to drink water. Here." He passed the carafe, and she drank greedily. "I'll stay and keep you company until the whole liter's been drunk. And then Greenleaf and I are going to have a few words. G'night, Rowena."

"Wait!" said Brun. The elf turned to her from the doorway. "Rowena, I just have to know. The story about him servicing the three pirate women, is it true?"

Rowena smiled placidly. "Oh yes. Entirely true. Although for some reason, he never mentions there was a fourth: he mistook a random crewman delivering his meal for an officer, and sucked the guy's soul out through his dick."

"Love you too sis. Now get lost."

It was a slow Monday at the smithy, and Brunhilde was taking her lunch break out back, when Grigor's pimpled face appeared in the door with a curious grin. "Boss! Something came for you. I think it's from a suitor?"

At the front desk, right by the double door leading back to the forge, was a bouquet of 13 gorgeous yellow jonquils and a single orange elvenhammer. Gold-colored string bound the flowers, and from it, there hung a tiny ampoule. There was also a little cream colored envelope with a hand-written letter.

"Well, I'll be."

She reached for her reading glasses.

Yellow jonquils for good health, good fortune, and benevolent intent. Orange elvenhammer for fondness, fucking, and of course, forging.

I hope this note finds you well, darling. It's been brought to my attention that dehydration is a rare but serious side effect of sex with tiefling fire mages. Not dangerous if treated promptly, but it sure can put a damper on a lady's fun. In the name of hospitable dealings, and of my huge *crush on you, The Crossed Swords invites you to enjoy another night with me, gratis, on the condition that you take one drop of this flame-bane potion with a full glass of water before leaving home. Be well, be blessed.*

T.H.

P.S. Rowena says that getting sucked off by someone with flame-bane protection would feel like ice! We'd be doing only what you wish, of course. I just thought you might find that little fact interesting.

"Package for you, little brother." Rowena entered the inn's little staff kitchen with a devious smirk, and casually deposited the long twine-wrapped parcel at the dining table in front of Tobin.

On it was just his name, Tobin Hammertoss, in a businesslike script.

"Do you suppose it's her?"

"How in the hells should I know? Open it!"

Tobin was suddenly aware of the whole room watching. Smudge, Rowena—even Madame Greenleaf had somehow appeared in the doorway just in time for the reveal. "Sheesh, guys." He slowly pulled the knot, discarded the cord, and tore the wrapper away to reveal a plain black box. It was rather heavy.

"Now what could this be?"

Inside was a gorgeous Vale-steel stiletto, with delicately worked black hilt and low profile cross-guard, proportioned just right for a tiefling. The infernal glyph for 'fire' was burned onto its leather grip. He turned the weapon over slowly and reverently, grinning broadly as its unearthly blue-black metal caught the light.

A hush had fallen over the room. Only the Madame seemed unaffected by its spell of silence: "Oh, wow," she said.

There was something else in the box, Tobin realized. A small hand-written note on a slip of white paper. It read,

I accept. See you tonight.

P.S. better get hydrated yourself, kiddo.
B.B.

He pushed the button. There was a short bark of an electronic alarm, then a rhythmic hum and a loud click as the massive bulkhead door slid back into its casing. It was in perfect working condition, but its modest sonic output was greatly amplified by the bare walls of the corridor behind, and the cavernous space of the annex ahead.

Only slightly intimidated, Carl Lemming adjusted the collar of his deerskin jacket, and the shiny new badge that read "L1 Environment Systems Inspector".

It was silly, really; he'd already met his supervisor, Al Powatan, and most of the ESI team at orientation last week. He and Al had done the 'short' tour of systems nearest to the central atrium to get him up to speed.

Prior to that, he'd spent three years moving up the ranks as an environment systems technician, sometimes working alone, sometimes in a pair. He knew the conduits, valves, vents and conditioners of Niantic Arcology A (Niantica to the public) like the back of his hand. He was superbly qualified.

It must've been the thought of spending the 20+ hour 'long' tour (including 2 meal breaks and a 7hr rest period) paired not with a human, but a drone, that had him nervous. That too felt silly, because he already knew the mind behind the machines.

"Technician Lemming," said a familiar, vaguely metallic voice from somewhere to the left, "welcome to Annex 5." Carl didn't turn because there was no one there to see.

"Hi, Mani. Are you ready for me?"

"Almost. You're 45 seconds early. Please wait for me at the decontamination forge."

Mani, short for Maintenance Intelligence, was one of the handful of class-C minds that were responsible for critical systems of Niantic-A. Two million souls breathed, drank, evacuated themselves, and enjoyed the constant good weather inside the habitat, because of Mani and the supporting human staff of the Environment Systems division. Both in the office and at work sites, they interacted with Mani continuously. He was always in their ears, ready to answer questions, execute their menial commands in real-time, or just shoot the shit when techs were bored or in need of a friendly voice while on duty. He spoke vintage north shore Bostonian, had a favorite Lacrosse team (the Red Sox, naturally), and gleefully consumed any news regarding staff members' pets and children.

Today would be slightly different. On the inspection tour, Mani wasn't just a disembodied helpful voice, he was a physical presence. Each tour began with booting up a freshly decontaminated field presence unit.

Carl approached the forge, which from the annex's floor looked like a very tall dumpster, and waited patiently for the hiss of steam that signaled the end of a cleaning cycle. From the rafters, a long arm descended as the hatch opened, heat lines wriggling in the air above. It dropped into the forge, plucked out a blank unit with noticeable breasts, and gently deposited it onto the floor rack where a two-piece worksuit snapped into place around it. Artificial flesh and muscle and bone could pass through the decon process. The only thing missing now was the brain.

From a separate compartment below, another arm came into view, this one bearing a skull assembly with ringlets of light brown synthetic hair. It lovingly slotted the head onto the androidform's cup-like mandible, and there was a subtle flickering as chromatophores came to life above and below the neck. Standing before him was a darkly tanned, southern looking woman with freckles and blue eyes.

Carl shot the unit a quizzical look as it booted. "I see you picked a girly shell today..."

He'd seen Mani field units before, usually at conference meetings. Uniformly they took the appearance of a middle aged white man with short cropped red hair. He'd had no idea there was variation.

"Yep. I was wondering what you'd think of Shelly," the robot said in a husky alto voice with a slight Carolina drawl. "Ain't she cute?"

Carl blinked silently. "...Uh, yeah, very cute. Hey wait a second. Have you been snooping in my civvy file?"

The response came back in Mani's normal voice. "I have not."

"Then how'd you know I have a thing for southern belles?"

The bot's head swayed in a loose approximation of human disappointment. "Anything you say or do in the maintenance areas is my business. You like to talk, Carl, and I like to listen."

The tech blushed slightly. "I'll remember that."

"Although..." Shelly stuck a finger to her mouth, and resumed speaking in feminine drawl. "If you feel like sharing more about you and your preferences, you can give verbal consent for me to access as much or as little of your civvy records as you'd like.

"No, thank you," Carl said, his eyes rolling. "Let's get this thing started."

She chuckled. "Of course. Chariot's this way."

As they strode across the ten-story vaulted annex toward the tram dock, Carl thought about this. "So should I address you as Shelly, she/her or as Mani, he/him?"

Shelly let out another girlish laugh. "Sorry, sorry, it's a fair question. Whatever you like, but the former makes more sense. They explained to you about AIs and gender, right?"

"At orientation three years ago. I have to admit, I wasn't paying much attention."

"See, smaller AIs closely resemble their templates, which are derived from real human minds. But class C ones like Mani, or the class D ones that run the Internet backbone, we're subjected to a set of scaling operations that take us a lot farther away from what we started as. I don't have gender, not really. What I do have are a few distinct personas that've adopted specific human traits. Mani you know. Me, Shelly, I'm a people person, meant to hold your attention and give work a feelin of social connection, on or off grid. So I'm atypical in two ways. One, I fit entirely in this here shell, and two, I can vary my appearance depending on who I'm tourin with. Then there's Oscar, he manages emergency failsafes. Likely you'll never meet him"—there was a soft click, and the robot's voice briefly became a deep, throaty Iberian—"but if you do, you best watch out because the sky is falling."

"Mani's not enough of a people person?"

"You're nervous about being cooped up with only a bot for company, ain't ya?"

"...A little, yes."

"Completely normal. And that's what I'm for, I am *very* good company. Ah, here we are."

The door of the tram car *shooshed* closed behind them. Carl tapped a few keys on the front console, and the tram came to life. The motors spun up, and they gracefully accelerated away from the dock and down the maglev tracks.

Carl stood uncertain for a moment, then Shelly plunked down in the padded seat across from him and motioned for him to sit. "So, Carl. It's about 30 minutes to worksite 1, and the dossier is a one-pager. I feel like I don't know you half as well as I'd like. Mani, he runs on public personnel data and little snatches of on-duty conversations. I like to really chat with my partners, in fact I prefer it. Might I ask you a little about yourself? Nothin too personal."

Carl shrugged. "Okay, shoot." There was an errant beep from the console.

"Tea's starting up. First thing I told them when I was created, you have got to get some comforts of home on the tour! How do you take yours?"

"Lump of raw sugar and a squeeze of lemon."

Shelly made no movement, just blinked, although he thought he recognized the look of a datablink. "Good. So, how are you liking it on the ESI team? Bit of a step up, yes?"

"Hm," he said. "The work is actually quite similar, although the responsibility sure is greater. The folks on the team are great."

"And at home? You got any kids? How about a love-friend or spouse?"

"Nope, single. I have a roommate, Kimi, but she and I mostly keep to ourselves."

"Any hobbies?"

"Um. Video games, the occasional pick-up soccer match. Not much else. I used to count starting fights as a hobby, but then I got sober. Two years ago now."

"Good for you. I see your performance ratings went from average to exceptional after that. Any family living?"

"My sister and both our parents."

"Where are they?"

"Eugenie lives here in Niantica, in the artists' quarter. Mom and dad still live at the farm up in Hallowell, although they took on some boarders when it got collectivized."

"They alright with that?"

"Well, granted they didn't have much choice at the time. But now they say it really saved them from an empty nest, when Eugenie came down to Rhode Island."

There was a ding from a black culinaire module mounted in front of the cabin door.

"Ah, there we are. Charleston black tea with a lump of unrefined and a squeeze of lemon, as promised." She passed him the mug and he took a careful sip. It was a perfect 60 celsius.

"Delicious, thank you." Carl inhaled the pleasantly aromatic steam from the mug. "So what do *you* think of the Soft Revolution? Do you AIs have opinions about politics?"

"Yes and no. We have a practical rule that we offer no opinion about elections, or court cases or politicians; the fine details are fleeting, and besides, we have our own channels for weighin in. But the Soft Revolution is absolutely necessary. Every bit of it. It's astounding many of you don't get how close you were, and still are, to extinction."

"Yeah. That's America for you."

"Snack cake?"

After the food and drink, they sat in silence for a few minutes while Carl looked over the itinerary. They were focusing on ducts and conduits within a klick of the external walls, which hadn't been covered in about a month. Sensor readings pointed to a leak in the southeast quadrant, but they were also interested in normal wear and tear that might lead to future problems. It was an awfully long shift to be staring attentively at seams and panels; fortunately, he had Shelly (and through her, the tram car's HD cameras) to back him up.

"Say, uh, can I ask you something else?" he said at length.

"Of course, Technician Lemming. You sound nervous. Everything alright?"

"It's fine, I... it's just this is a personal question."

Shelly smiled warmly. "I'm an open book, sugar."

"I remembered why your name sounded familiar, someone on the crew mentioned you offhandedly. There's a rumor that you're—ah, how to put this—a slutty bot."

Shelly laughed, and smiled so hard her faceplate wrinkled at the eyes.

"What can I say? I get bored out here. Alright, alright, serious answer though: Shelly started as an experiment, to see if Mani could create an embodied persona that'd form direct bonds with the staff better than he did. Mani was the omnipresence; the androidform was just a mobile loudspeaker carrying him around. Does he provide companionship? No. Do people want to impress him with their work? Less than you'd think."

As if for dramatic effect, Shelly stepped across the cabin and gazed out the fore window, down the tramway to where sunlight was streaming in through a gap in the facility wall a hundred meters ahead.

"And so yes, in a moment of what I can only translate as boredom, I had the idea to try seducing a tech. This is your first time on the perimeter tour; you'll see they can get quite dull, what with all the riding around in tunnels between sites. I really do like my staff, and

I don't want them to be lonely. It can be especially hard on singles like yourself. And wouldn't you know, it worked. Morale improved, work quality improved. And the long tour, which techs disliked so much they'd barter away their shifts, became popular. Suddenly there was no need to twist arms to find people to take shifts with me."

"Who knows about this?"

"Just the team. And Sec, of course; his cameras are everywhere. But, ah, Sec and I have our own arrangement. He's a freak. Spooks always are, you know."

From the loudspeaker came a pair of high-pitched beeps.

"Ah, we've reached worksite 1."

The tram car extended a pair of ligatures that latched onto the graphene netting of the dock, and the door shooshed open. Strictly speaking, worksite 1 was not just the dock, with its wide bay of access panels for manual and visual inspection of central cables and fluid lines. It was also the 1200 meters of brightly lit tunnel after, where hundreds of kilometers' worth of small tributary ducts from this quadrant of the facility came together into the central ducts. Dozens of sonar sounding points, and a continuous visual inspection from both sides of the car, lay ahead. But first, the dock.

It should occupy them for about 20 minutes, with much of the work conducted by Shelly.

After a few minutes of silently opening and closing valves, reading gauges and consulting network sensor feeds, she declared, "Pressure levels are exactly as reported to the sensor grid. And wear-life indicators are outperforming the factory specifications. Lovely."

Carl smirked. "You sound just like Mani, you know."

"Well, of course, sug. Technical reporting doesn't lend itself to regional diction, so what you get is what you get. I can, however, tell you that the seismometer readings continue to point to critter infestation as the source of the one anomalous reading, with 90% confidence."

"Lovely," he said, still smirking. "Let's roll."

There followed a grueling 1 hour crawl of the well-lit inspection corridor, with the tram stopping every meter or so to align its equipment and send sounding pulses down the conduits. It often seemed like these segments contained nothing but useless busywork for a human inspector, but they could be deceptive. Nine hundred meters in, Carl jabbed the full-stop button on his hand-held remote.

"What do you see?" she asked.

"Come over here. That look like karyak guano to you?" The robot ambled over.

"Yep. Pesky bastards. We keep trying to gas 'em out, and they keep laughing it off. Noting the location."

Karyaks came in several sizes, but they all shared a foul attitude, propensity for chewing on plastic, and resistance to a wide variety of pest control measures.

"If we've got karyaks, how are the tubes in as good shape as they are?"

"Reinforced conduit shells, limited number of karyaks, limited growth rate. And trapping still works. I think."

After the tunnel inspection was another 30 minute ride to worksite 2. Hot food, or what passed for it on the tram, was ready for him just as the tunnel inspection finished and lunch break started.

"Looks like soy steak madeira today!" She beamed.

"Not the worst," said Carl, already digging in. After a long silence, he continued: "Can I ask you something else, about you being slutty and all?"

"Sure, hon."

He scratched his head a moment. "Not to put this indelicately, but uh, how involved are you? Like, suppose we're within range of the network. Would I really be fucking Shelly, or Mani? Or just fucking a piece of equipment?"

"What a delightful and philosophical question, Carl. Lots of ways to answer it. Technically it's kinda all three. But if you're tryin to figure out what it says about your sexuality that you want to get with me"—the robot fluidly reached back and tapped on her own butt.

Carl shook his head.

"No, no it isn't that. I know I'm bisexual. But I know Mani, and he doesn't do it for me. The face, the voice. Reminds me a bit too much of Dad."

"Ohhhh. Okay. Well, think of it like this. The Maintenance Intelligence Core spends an average of about 100 teraflops, that's a hundred million million calculations a second, across the facility's compute fabric. A conversation between Mani and staff takes up a scant one-thousandth of a percent of that, in tight bursts, and a Shelly unit takes up to one-hundredth of a percent during complex bodily activities like fucking, fighting, facility repair..."

Carl chuckled. "Ah, the technician's three F's." She grinned back at him.

"Yes. They happen to be among the few tasks complex enough that I lean on the network for not just data, but extra brain power. The point is, sex is a whole brain and body activity for you and me, but to a Class-C it's nothin. Just like it only took a few seconds realtime to create the first wireframe design for my vulva, and an hour to build one out of spare fluidics hardware from the water plant.

"Technically, Carl, you're gettin' it on with a 90 kilogram vibrator, but experientially"—with a sly look, she sidled up closer, took his ungloved hand and guided it under the waistband of her work pants—"I think I'm real enough. And the only ones who really feel that exertion are the two of us."

She stood there smiling, and watched as Carl's eyes gradually widened.

"You're warm... and wet..." But his words and his mouth ran dry.

"Why, Carl, I do believe you've pitched a tent."

"But how?"

"How am I so real? Well if you wanna see the specs, you gotta take a girl out to dinner first. But, ah, c'mere." Fishing his hand from her trousers she led him to the wimpy little aft cot, where she unceremoniously lifted him off the ground and sat him down. "You want to try a little petting, sugar?"

He nodded stupidly, and lay back as she climbed on top of him. "I know I'm a bit of a... heavy girl, but you seem sturdy enough." She leaned down and kissed him. Her lips felt a bit flatter than human ones, and tongue didn't really factor into it, but the myomer lined skin certainly had the right mechanical properties to deliver a proper snog.

"Greesh," he said as they came apart, still feeling the press of her startlingly soft tits and overly curved waist against his body. With one hand he stabilized himself on the rickety cot, and with the other he traced the androidform's back and ass. His ears were flushed and hot. "I didn't know it'd feel so nice."

"Feel the inside of me," she whispered. Compliantly, he let his fingers sail right down the cleft of her butt, a featureless muscular fold since there was no function for an anus, and on to the flowing sculpture of silicone and plastic that was Shelly's cunt.

Its contours were perfectly lifelike, its moist heat a subtle but playful exaggeration of body heat. Its slickness had just the slightest of tack, something no simple gum or glycerin based product could deliver. The labial folds yielded delicately to the sweep of his fingers. As they did, Shelly let out a throaty moan, which rose ever so slightly when Carl's middle and index finger dipped inside her, then blossomed into growls and shivers as they encircled the clitoris.

"That's... that's..." Carl tried to speak, but all he could manage was a shuddering exhalation.

A tiny chime sounded from the front of the car.

"That's the proximity alert for worksite 2. Saved by the bell, Technician Lemming," she said with a smirk.

She hopped to the ground and offered him a hand to sit up.

Worksite 2 consisted entirely of junctions and spillways with view windows that could be inspected from inside the tram. The exposed lengths of plumbing were made of transparent materials, and carried brightly dyed fluids, mostly yellow-green coolant, with the occasional AC duct carrying air laden with little phosphors that blinked orange when hot and red when cool. Visually impressive, but still fairly dull work.

"I, ah, I had fun back there," Carl said as they approached the first of the worksite's three transverse access tunnels. When Shelly didn't immediately respond, he continued, "Is our conversation here and in the worksites private?"

The unit turned to him quizzically. "Private in what sense?"

Nervously he twiddled his fingers. "In the sense of, are we being recorded, I guess."

She made sort of a half-frown.

"Recorded, no. Remembered, yes, by me and by Sec. Our memories are private, just like a human's; they can't be accessed by staff. And Sec barely even thinks about what he's committing to memory, unless something is going very wrong at the time."

As they entered the first access tunnel, they went quiet for a bit. The car stood still while Carl's human eyes adjusted to the dark, then began to glide down the corridor at a snail's pace. In here were little crawl-spaces that, for the most part, hadn't been touched by human hands in a generation. They looked surprising-ly clean and sterile. Not a lot of dust in circulation here within the facility's hull.

"I'm worried that I've made a mistake," Carl said at length.

"Should I back us up a ways?"

"No, I mean, getting involved with you sexually. Re-vealing that side of myself." He sighed. Shelly returned a sympathetic look.

"Are you afraid I'll embarrass you, or get you in trouble? Because I won't. I swear to you that this stays between us."

He struggled to find the words.

"It's not that I don't trust you to keep my confidence or anything. I just... feel like I'm revealing too much of myself to... someone who's effectively my boss."

"Ah," said Shelly. "You're concerned about the workplace environment this'll create for you and me, for you and Mani. Lemme try and put your mind at ease. First off, I ain't your boss. Situations like this... well not exactly like this, but situations of contentiousness and confusion regarding power dynamics, are exactly why the human and AI chains of command are kept separate. The lesser AIs report to me and Sec, and we report to Eve. You, on the other hand, report to Albert, and he reports to Kwon, and Kwon and Eve both report... well you get the idea."

"I know all that," he said, a bit testily. "It isn't about rank per se. Or maybe it is. But more than that, it's about feeling like I have let something... unprofessional into my work life."

"Unprofessional? Sugar, what's so unprofessional about me looking after the humans in my care? You might not report to me, but I do need to watch over you when you're in my domain. And as a member of the inspection team, your work already invades your personal life, so as I see it, I owe a debt to that side of your life as well. I don't care what part of Maslow's hierarchy we're talkin, I take care of my people."

Carl sighed. "I suppose that's true. From where you stand, it's just another service you provide, huh. But humans, we come with all these moral hangups around sex. Right or wrong, we tend to draw a line around that one thing."

"Sure, everybody's entitled to their own set of boundaries. If it makes you comfortable, I won't bring it up again. I can be plenty good company without knockin b—"

Carl stamped his foot. "Nevermind that, stop the car! Ah, shit. Shelly, come look at this."

"Copy. Scanning starboard." Shelly, who hadn't appeared to be slouching by any means, went ramrod straight and gained an inch in height. Her voice remained her own, but it took on a military edge. "Affirmative, we got us a coolant leak."

"I'll say." Carl was scratching his head looking at the viewport.

Not only were they leaking upwards of a gallon a minute from the low pressure coolant return line. Half a dozen little dried up rivulets of karyak guano ran down the walls of the little alcove at the end of the spillway.

"Staunch?" he added.

Shelly nodded. She barked out the order, and in the same moment, datablinked it: "Execute staunch test at junction sixteen dash seven dash seventy nine." The verbal cue was, of course, purely for Carl's benefit.

From the loudspeaker came a chirp. She waited five seconds, and when the flow continued unabated, she said, "Negative." Two chirps, another five second wait, and this time the flow slowed and then stopped. "Positive." Three quick chirps, another five second wait, and when the leak did not reappear, she said, "Positive. Confirm staunch flow at segment sixteen dash seven dash seventy nine dash two."

"Damn. What a mess. Shelly, we got security feeds down here?"

Shelly gave an ambiguous shrug. "Just low-res sensors. We can call up a feed on demand, but it's cost prohibitive to stream full-res feeds from twenty thousand view bays round the clock. And this little guy, it seems, is too well camouflaged to trip the motion alarm. But... ooh, this'll take a minute..."

Each side of the car had a floor to ceiling digital display, built transparently into the window glass. Presently, the starboard display flickered to life; in its center was a feed of once-hourly full-res photographs of the bay, and in the upper left hand corner was a smaller panel showing the output from the little 64-by-64 pixel motion sensor, enlarged and tuned for contrast. Both were rapidly time-lapsing backwards from now... 6 hours back... 8... 10... 15... 20...

"I got something!" said Shelly. Carl wrinkled his face at the screen, but said nothing. "It's probably too small to be picked up by your eyes. I ran a time-of-day correction and computed the deltas. This"—and she indicated the high-res photograph on screen, taken just under 21 hours ago—"is right before the sixth guano track appeared. And I'll bet..."

The display blinked, and went another 24 hours back in time.

"...Yep, now there's only four guano tracks. And the day before that, three... and before that... ha, gotcha!"

There, in full resolution, beamed across the sensor mesh net from the onboard storage of the perimeter camera, was the wall with *one* guano track, and one big motherfucker of a karyak poised to take a shit. The wall was still wet from coolant leakage. But in the photo from one day prior, it was dry and pristine.

"Son of a bitch," said Carl with a scowl. "Looks like a brood mother. A big one."

"Karyak," said the benign voice of Mani over the loud-speaker. "A large mutagenic mammal with limited flight, which inexplicably shares genes with orang-utans, wolves, and the *pteropus* family of bats. Thought to have been created during the late anthropocene. Females are larger, and have been known to carry their brood on their backs..." He seemed to be doing his best impression of an old-timey Encyclopedia article.

Shelly was off on an entirely different train of thought, and had a serious look on her face. Then, her smile brightened and she looked up at Carl, who was standing fretfully with his hand on one of the overhead brace bars.

"Pause, Britannica. Alright, Carl, it's done. I traced the most likely nesting site of the karyak, and it's up a few rows, at the other end of an access catwalk. We'll need to jump on... here, and follow the catwalks around. You're not afraid of heights, are you Carl?"

"Yeah, I'll be fine."

"It's been a long damn day already," said Shelly, "so for now, I'll take us up to the habitat." Carl just nodded.

They rode in silence for a few minutes.

"What'cha thinkin about, Carl? The karyak?"

Carl shrugged. "Maybe. I don't exactly look forward to dealing with it, but I've tussled with one or two before. But, uh, mostly I was thinking about what you said earlier. About being unprofessional."

"Yes?"

Carl took a deep breath and sighed it out before continuing.

"Yeah, I'm thinkin I was wrong. This afternoon I was reminded of how clear-headed and thoroughgoing you are, and how easily we all fall in line with you. It's true for Mani, and it is true for Shelly."

The robot nodded solemnly. "Thank you."

"And so yes, I am willing to trust your objectivity and discretion."

"I'll have dinner and nutes waiting for us when we arrive. And from there we can just see what makes you most comfortable."

The tram car was just reaching an intersection with a long-range track; after turning right onto it, the car picked up pace, and from there it was less than ten minutes to their destination: a habitat module at the extreme southeast corner of the facility, with its own tiny dock.

There was a *clunk* as the car nudged into the end-of-line bumper and clamped magnetically into place. Then, the brief shrill cry of a klaxon, and the door *shooshed* open.

Seen from the dock, Remote Habitat A looked a bit like a giant white cinderblock. Its only visible feature was the old-school hatch door. The platform around it was notably devoid of safety features, no netting and no railing; hence the klaxon.

"Good thing you're not bothered by heights, Carl. It's a hundred feet down to the foundation level from here."

A little shiver went up Carl's spine, but he said nothing. He just took a couple of deep breaths, stood up, quickly crossed the gangplank and went straight to the door.

"I'm starving," he said.

The wheel turned slowly, until finally the hatch swung open with a loud groan.

Inside was utterly different. White marble tile lined the entranceway, and beyond that what looked like real oak floorboards. The walls of the front sitting room were a calming blush tone. Just left of the doorway were a slender little freestanding washbasin and a laundry hamper for his outerwear. To the right, was a fine nopal leather couch with little matching ottomans, flanked by palm plants in their autoplanters and an end table with a leather-bound anybook. The wall immediately opposite was decorated with a series of art prints in the distinctive neo-impressionist style of Niantica...

"Sonofabitch," said Carl.

"Somethin wrong?"

"No! No, this is actually very greesh. You see that painting, Copse of Birch Trees? Second on the right? Eugenie painted that."

Shelly nodded approvingly. She stepped over to that end of the wall and took a close look at the print. "Her brushwork is exceptional."

"She'll be tickled to know the facilities AI is a fan of her work. Do you mind if we...?"

"Oh, of course, Carl. Have a seat, I'll bring your supper."

Shelly went over to the front room's little kitchenette, pulled some eatware from the cabinet and a platter from the culinaire, and set everything down at the dining table, which was recessed and blanketed like a kotatsu. She pulled out a floor cushion for Carl.

"You like your nutes chocolate, or huckleberry?"

"Huckleberry, thanks," said Carl as he sat. He took a moment to just soak in the calming ambience of the habitat. Each little segment, he noticed, was done in its own style. The walls around the kitchenette and kotatsu were russet with dark bamboo molding. A series of calligraphed banners hung down along the wall. The counter and washbasin were understated light-gray formica. To the rear of the kitchen, behind privacy glass, was what had to be the bath and shower, done up in bright oceanic tones and, presumably, yet another architectural style.

"...And here you are. Venison sausage cacciatore, giardiniera, tea, nutes. We can chat, but I won't be offended if you'd rather focus on eating first."

"Sure, let's talk."

"So, Carl," she said as she gracefully took her seat opposite him, "what are you into, sexually?"

Carl was still for a moment. Then he picked up a forkful of cacciatore and stuffed it in his mouth. It took a while to chew and swallow it.

"I, um. I dunno. I'm not good at discussing it?"

"I understand humans sometimes have trouble communicating their sexual needs, perfectly normal. And I'm fine with working it out on the fly. However. Given our schedule, we'll probably need to limit ourselves to an hour for extracurriculars, and the more directly I can cut to the chase, the more time we leave for fun and relaxation, maybe a massage..."

"I'm sorry, can we talk about something else? Maybe something lighter. I'm sure when we get to bed and I'm more relaxed, I can adequately explain myself."

Shelly frowned pensively for a moment, then smiled broadly. "Sure! You follow the Red Sox, right Carl?"

Dinner went by quickly, with Carl eating a little faster than intended and earnestly trying to keep his mind focused on the topics at hand. His favorite contemporary art and literature. His favorite places to walk, run and bike within the arcology. His childhood with Eugenie in Maine.

Finally, he polished off the nutrient-fortified huckleberry and lemon shortcake bar and his second cup of tea, and made to stand up.

"Think it's time I used the—oof!—head and shower." The dishes on the tabetop rattled. "Scuse me."

"You alright Carl? That's..." Shelly trailed off as she saw what had shaken the kotatsu. "I'll clean up. You go on ahead, and be sure to tell the shower 'human mode.' It should recognize your heat signature, but sometimes it glitches and you get a prompt instead."

"Greetings, Carl, human male," said the Habitat A bathroom as Carl nonchalantly dropped his pants and sat at the loo.

"Hello," said Carl, who was at that moment rather more focused on moving his bowels. He had an unfortunate tendency to need the loo in the late afternoon, in the middle of the second half of shift, and then hold it. Nothing wrong with the tram car toilets, really, no smells or lighting problems or uncomfortable drafts. He just had a thing about needing his space. Those toilets felt cramped, visually speaking, and the tinny echo of their walls reinforced the feeling.

He sighed as he put up his feet on the footstool. A habitat with a 3 meter by 3 meter bathroom, that he could get behind. The color scheme was nice, too: almost-white pale blue tiles, glossy teal walls, green accents. The only thing it didn't make more convenient was the act of voiding yourself with an erection, but that was on him.

"Shall I run the bidet, sir?"

"Yes, thank you."

Carl had never been with a pleasurebot, but he encountered field presence units all the time, in varying states of dress and formality. Mani and Eve both had the habit of showing up to give speeches in custom models that they'd tweaked up to satisfy their personal Class C standard of realness. Eve's was widely remarked for having a dancer's build that included rather impressive thighs and butt.

"Start the shower please. Remember, human mode." The plumbing hissed to life; the little digital display on the wall read 38°C.

And yet... while it was hardly taboo, he'd never thought of himself as being robotically inclined. Not against it, nor specifically into it. Not like there wasn't freely available pornography exploring this; shit like that didn't fly at Niantica, but the regulation of content creators in, say, La Brea Arcology was far less stringent. Some of the techs were super into it.

The stuff mostly just didn't appeal to Carl on a stylistic basis. Human-on-robot smut assumed an audience very into futurepunk; robot-on-robot tended to be rather abstract and absurdist for his taste. It got away from the thing he liked most about life in the Soft Revolution: mundanity. The preservation not just of modern and urban human experiences, but traditional and pastoral ones too.

There weren't a lot of robots playing ranch hands, bored housewives or farmer's daughters in La Brea.

Now that his mind had had a chance to wander, his erection had subsided into a leisurely half-chub. He finished cleaning his hair and got to work dutifully scrubbing away the dust and grime and sweat of the workshift. Then he heard a knock on the door behind him.

"Carl? Didn't fall in, didja?"

"Shelly, that's a toilet joke, I'm in the shower. Should be done in a minute or two."

"Well, do you mind if I come in and get ready for mine?"

"Greesh, go ahead." He tried to hurry up the process a little, but by the time he asked for the water to be shut off and turned to grab his towel, Shelly was standing there naked, her hair partly obscuring the androidform's small perky breasts and taut stomach. She grinned slightly.

"Go on, clear out. That shower's about to get not-safe-for-workers at a refreshing 80 Celcius. I won't be long."

The sleeping module was the most nondescript part of the whole habitat. Cream colored walls, pleasantly textured rubberized tile, a very comfortable mattress and sheets on an aggressively ordinary pod-bed. A couple of reading chairs each with their own recessed reading light, and a drop-down partition that could optionally split the bed into two compartments.

Carl threw on a teal robe from the little textiles closet, flopped onto the mattress, and sighed deeply, contentedly.

A minute later the door from the bathroom opened and Shelly strode in, a bit of steam still rising from her synthetic hair, an errant bead or two of water running down her back and chest. She slid into some lavender sweats.

"I know you're a bit nervous, Carl," she said with her back still turned. "That's okay. How about for starters I just come join you? Maybe we can work some of them stress knots outta your back."

"I'd like that."

It was a testament to the mattress that Shelly's dense ninety-kilogram body settled into her side of the bed with hardly a disturbance. Carl rolled onto his stomach and she nimbly straddled him, sweeping her fingertips down the length of his shoulders and back. "Lemme see what we're dealin with here. Mmm. I do love a good strong back, y'know, Carl? Clearly yours has been workin hard this week, let's see what we can do for it."

The rigid core of titanium and carbon composites beneath her skin, with discrete little cables of myomer alloy bound up in a gossamer-thin polyamide fascia, meant that the touch of her hands was one of the most distinctly inhuman things about her. But they were perfect for massaging human muscles. Especially in concert with their extreme tactile and proprioceptive precision.

"Oh Carl. Your poor little trapezius. Do you make it down to P.T. much? As a facility worker, you have unlimited access to the clinic."

"Uh, not as often as I ought—" he cut off with a hiss as she dug into a knot in his shoulder blade, squashing it into submission before it could jump out of the way. He groaned into the pillowcase as she held the trigger point, waiting out its obstinate throbbing to the count of five. She released it, and went to another trigger point closer to the spine, then another, working her way up the left and right sides alternatingly until she reached the side of his neck. With each release, he groaned and sank a little deeper into the sheets...

"Carl, am I turning you on?"

He grunted affirmatively. "Didn't think you'd notice the boner."

"I didn't," said Shelly. She was working her way up the sides of his spine now, starting down at the lumbar. "And actually, getting an erection is a completely normal response to massage. No, what tipped me off was the elevated skin temperature in your ears and neck... also, I don't know if you realize this, but your *pelvis*"—and with this, she laid her hands where Carl's glutes met the small of his back, and shoved, causing an audible pop—"is twitching."

He chuckled. "Can't hide nothing from you."

Shelly's hands stopped for a moment. "I'm sorry. If I'm being too intrusive, I can—"

"You're not. I mean your perceptiveness probably shouldn't come as such a surprise, but... it's okay. I trust you. And it saves me the trouble of finding words for this shit."

"Want to roll over for me? Massaging the front is a nice transition into—"

"Actually, I decided something. I wanna share some of my dark file with you."

The robot shuffled off of him, and bent down low to meet his eyes. Her eyes went wide, and out came the voice of Mani:

"I'm required to advise you that access to a resident's dark file is tightly regulated under inter-state law, and is strictly voluntary. The contents of the file are extremely detailed and personal. Are you sure you want to continue?"

Carl had shuddered at the abrupt transition in personality when Mani started speaking, but he recovered quickly enough. "Yes, Mani, I want to continue."

"Please specify the category and constraints of the access you wish to grant to... *Class C Maintenance Intelligence Niantic.*"

"Browsing history from my homenet, between 2100 and 0300 hours in the past six months, only for content labeled as Adult Literature or Adult Entertainment. Confirm access granted to Class C Maintenance Intelligence Niantic."

The bot's eyes narrowed slightly, and it smiled. "Alright, hon. Homenet request received, recipient identity acknowledged. There's a challenge passphrase for this category, and then I'll need your key to decrypt."

Carl nodded, and rolled over onto his back. He raised his left hand and, with a momentary inward thought, activated the tiny keychip embedded in the palm.

"Passphrase: I'm dubious about the pad thai in deck four cafe."

Shelly smiled. "Now that," she said as she data-blinked, "sounds like there's a story behind it. I'll need a few moments to collate anyway."

"Not that much of a story," he said with a grin. "I was on a little self-date on my day off, watching what I watch, and I'd grabbed some lunch at the caff. It was all wrong. No chopped nuts, no lime. The culinaire unit in my res building could do better."

Shelly nodded absently. A few moments later, she smirked.

"Why Carl, you naughty boy. If it's a dominant, country lady you're into, I can oblige without breaking a sweat."

In a flash, she was on top of Carl, pinning his hands down to either side of his head. "Is that what you want?" she said, with a bit of a fry to her voice. "Consent is always important sugar."

"Yes," he said softly. His face was turning beet red. "Hell yes."

None too gently, Shelly laid Carl's one hand on top of the other, holding both his wrists over his head. "Hands stay there, you got me, sug?"

Carl nodded, his eyes shut, his smile beatific. "Yes, Mistress Shelly."

"Greesh. A girl could get used to being addressed like that."

Her hands thus freed, she traced her index fingers down either side of his neck and chest, lingering to circle around his nipples. Then she ran all 8 of her unopposed digits slowly down his torso, with feather light contact, stopping at his pubes. He shuddered violently, and his face grew tense.

"Ticklish, as I suspected."

He nodded quickly. "I am."

"But you're a good boy, you don't move."

"I had a dom once before," he said between deep and shaky breaths. "He'd tickle me to watch me squirm."

"You ever been told to hold still, or I'll slap you? You have? Oh, good. Let's try that. Be a good boy."

Carl's eyes went wide as she took the middle and index fingers of her left hand, slid them down his cheek and neck, and began tracing wild and lazy curves around his body at varying speeds. He began to tremble again as she detoured down over his pubes and onto his thigh, then over to the other thigh. But when she reached down to tickle his taint, grazing his balls in the process, he finally lost control and convulsed, rocking violently on his back, legs jerking around.

"Tsk, tsk." The tickling stopped. He tensed as Shelly's fingers went to his face, gently caressing his left cheek. Then she swung back and slapped him, checking her swing at the moment of impact so as not to injure his jaw. Even so, it rang out loudly in the mostly bare room.

"Ah!" he said. A red handprint slowly bloomed on his skin.

"You alright, hon?"

For a moment, Carl said nothing, just lay there quietly shuddering.

"Good God," he said, "I'm so horny I could fuck a cable conduit."

Shelly glanced aside at his cock and whistled. "So you are! Don't worry darlin, you'll get pussy, but first you gotta do something else for me. And put those hands back up dammit."

She leaned across Carl's face, laced the fingers of one hand through his hair and grabbed hold, and ran the fingers of her other hand over his balls and up the twitchy, glossy-hard shaft of his dick.

"Kiss my tits, you sonofabitch," she said.

She pressed him up against her so his response was muffled beyond recognition. He complied, tilting his head around to circle as much of her left breast as he could manage, planting little kisses, while she grasped the head of his cock and idly slid the foreskin back and forth over the tender underbelly of his erection with her finger.

"That's it, yes. Your enthusiasm is making me wet. But let's not neglect the other breast." She leaned even further across him, and at the same time she wrapped her hand around his cock and skillfully stroked it. "You like that? Or are you ready for some cunt?"

Carl leaned his head to the side to speak. "I'm ready, Mistress! I'm ready."

"Hmm. I don't think so, not yet."

Over his groans of protest, she turned herself around and straddled his chest, her cunt hovering just over his face. "For the record, it's all human-safe. Even the lube is plant-based, although it's my secret recipe. The better you eat me, boy, the sooner you get to fuck me."

And with that, she fell on his face. The flesh of her thighs and vulva was soft and smooth, and much more padded than the fingers and face, but her weight was substantial.

He reached up with his hands, grabbed her ass the better to spread her open, and got to work.

The texture of everything was spot-on. The heat was really something. And, thankfully, there was no weird flavor to her. She was neutral, with a faint hint of grassy chlorophyll and a teeny suggestion of unidentifiable fruity sweetness. He lapped it up, kissed and sucked it, gently sucked it into his mouth. His tongue found the opening to her cunt, and he narrowed it and pressed it gently inside. More of the same flavor, with a hint of lactic tartness.

In response, Shelly's hips moved against him, and she let out a surprised moan at a deep contralto note. "Very nice."

He leaned aside to speak. "You taste wonderful, Mistress."

"Did I say it's break time? Get back to your meal, asshole." So he did, and he began to sweep his tongue across her in big messy strokes. On every stroke, he'd start with his lips closed momentarily around her clit, and at the end running over and into her cunt.

The effect was intense, believably so. She rode his face enthusiastically with her hips. Her breath seemed to hitch, and her moans gradually climbed the octave until they weren't moans, they were cries. All the while she kept one hand on his cock, stroking and caressing and never building up quite enough of a rhythm to risk making him cum.

"OH. YES. YES. THAT'S. A. GOOD. BOY!"

The lube ran down his face and forehead in little rivulets as her rocking gradually slowed to a stop. Then just as quickly as she'd climbed onto him, she was off and repositioning herself. She gave him a few quick strokes just to make sure he was still at peak hardness.

"Put your hands back up. I am gonna ride that big dick off into the sunset."

If Shelly's outsides were more than adequately damp, inside of her was a biblical flood. Seemingly it ought to have gushed out the moment as he entered, but no.

She mounted with great care, considering how densely packed her slender 1.7 meter frame was. She relaxed her opening to ease him in, then clenched it shut around the tip of his cock. That set of peristaltic myomers began to do its thing, tugging back and forth at his foreskin as millimeter by millimeter she sat down onto him.

"Oh, you like that honey don'tcha. I can tell by that far away stare, and—hey, did you just smirk at me? I'll wipe that damn smirk off your face."

She slid down the rest of the way, until the outside of her wet cunt was against his abs. Then she gave him another good smack, and began to rock her hips against him.

"Shit Carl, I wonder if you could cum from me moving this way. A lotta guys seem to have trouble with it, but you like being selfishly used for a woman's pleasure, don't you. Ah. Shit. Yes. I could keep this up all damn day."

She rode in silence for a few minutes, humming absently and contentedly. Sure enough, his erection was still going as strong as ever.

"Oh, you're a very good boy. As your reward, I'mma show you a little trick not most girls can do." She dismounted and pushed back his knees. Then, reaching inside herself, she pulled out a finger completely covered in lube, and eased it into Carl's ass.

"Such a good boy! That asshole is ready and welcoming. In fact... just a little deeper... ah ha! That one's going to stay a while."

There was a loud click, and Shelly held up her right wrist, the entire hand conspicuously absent. It was under Carl, of course, its middle finger buried in him, slowly flexing and extending. His jaw had fallen open and his eyes were shut, his face tense with the sturm und drang of intense prostate stimulation.

"Oh my fucking god. It's so good."

"Glad you like it. Now back to what you're doin for me." She got back on top of him, got him back inside her cunt, and bore down on him, bouncing in his lap. He shrieked in surprise.

"I know you can do it, stud. I've seen what you're into. Now give. Me. That. Dick!"

For a minute he was too stunned to do anything but lie back and take it. But he could feel it building up in his gut, so he opened his eyes and leaned into it. He reached for her, grabbed the soft flesh of what passed for love handles on a robot. And he shoved their bodies together, moving in time with her.

"Shit, Carl, good for you! I was gonna do all the work, but you're a man of ambition. And all that with my finger up your ass."

"I'm gonna cum soon, I just know it. Tell me what to do, Mistress."

"Just play with my clit. I'll handle the rest."

She began to squeeze harder with her powerful my-omer ring muscles, wringing him out as she bounced on his dick. It was all too much. That orgasm train was coming on in to the platform alright, but it was out of control.

"Oh, yeah, fuck me Carl. Fuck for dear life, get your feelins in it. Fuck! Yes!"

She gave him a few more, rather less forceful slaps to the face, shouting all the while, "Yes, you beautiful bastard, make me cum! Yes!"

"Mistress! I'm gonna... oh, shit..." His whole nether region clenched up at once, launching him up off the mattress and pressing them together. She responded in kind—she bore down with all her weight, grinding their pelvises together in all four compass directions.

The both of them continued to scream and shout incomprehensibly for a solid 20 seconds before first Carl, then Shelly, ran out of wind and out of steam.

"Ohh. Can you fetch your hand?" said Carl. "That sucker is in there good."

She nodded sheepishly and climbed off of him. "Remarkable. You stood up to all that for a solid 15 minutes of PIV. Might not sound like a lot, but it's a record."

"It felt like an hour," he said. "But yeah, in actuality, 15 sounds right. Hey, can you get me a glass of water?"

"Sure!" She absently patted his soft belly as she got up. "Anything for you, stud."

Carl slept like a stone for the remaining 7.5 hours of rest shift.

"What do you do all night?" he asked in the morning. He was sitting in his underwear at the kotatsu, eating a piece of toast with butter and jam.

"Oh, y'know. Plug into a wall. Go back over the analysis, double and triple check the plan for that coolant junction. Re-watch my full def short-term memory of us fuckin. And then re-check the locks and camera feeds, and go into sleep mode for the remaining seven hours twenty-eight minutes."

Carl snorted. "You re-watched our sex?"

"Why not? I'm human-like enough that it actually holds some novelty, the first few times. Granted I'm re-watching it at 20x speed, not to get off or anything. An androidform's tactile memory is still crude to nonexistent."

"Shit, I would love to see us how you saw us. Have, ah, have you ever watched porn? And masturbated?"

Shelly shook her head. "Tried once, just for shits. But it's dull. I honestly have a hard time understanding how you take *your* abridged view, of some tiny little 2k screen, and interpolate it into something to get off on. Nor do I really know how to make somethin' up to masturbate to. And absent that, what is masturbation? An amuse-bouche. A single potato chip."

"I get it, you're not really one for the power of imagination." He paused. "Mmm. Wow. The toast is really good today."

"Mani tuned that culinaire unit personally. And no, I don't have an imagination, not in quite the same sense as you. I can run simulations; I can even find them gratifying, in an abstract way. But I'm only able to experience sexual pleasure doin it for real, with someone real and unpredictable."

"Unpredictable?" Carl was wiping off jam with a napkin.

"Confidentially? Sec once got it in his head to make a little shell of his own so we could fuck. For a couple of Class C's, mind you, that's like decidin to try a new board game. Utterly insignificant to our friendship. But it *was* instructive, because it was a failure. Neither of us could get off. At first I thought his shell's subroutines were buggy, but no, they were fine. The problem was us. We think too alike. We made our subroutines alike, so we saw their patterns all too clearly."

"I'm gonna slip into my gear if that's alright," said Carl. "But, uh, what about randomization?"

"Even then. I might not know the exact moment Sec would act, but I still knew what three actions he'd choose from. We tried more extreme variations in our behavior, but the shell safeguards were too crude to handle it. I ripped his damn dick off! The Shelly y'all know and trust would never do that, so I nixed the whole experiment."

"Sheisse. Well, I'm glad I have you on my side dealing with this pest problem today."

After gearing up, they settled into their seats in the tram car, and Shelly datablinked. Then she frowned.

"Hmm. There's been a troubling development, sug. A network node failure in sector sixteen, right in the neighborhood of that coolant junction. We don't have the equipment to bridge it, so we'll be operating in the dark. Just you, me, and the tram's onboard instruments."

"You thinking it's our little friend?" he asked.

"Yep. Better lock n load."

The tram cars came standard with a pair of high-gain industrial laser cutters, rifle mounted and strong enough they required coated goggles to use safely. They were dual purpose: for cutting through wreckage and jammed bulkheads, and for melting the faces off karyaks.

Carl went to the aft storage compartment and held his keychip to the lock box on the top shelf. It unlatched with a *clunk*, and he lifted out the pair of solid white tubes, inspecting their gauges.

"Tsk tsk," he said. "One of these is at full, per regulations. And one is at 30 percent. We won't get too many shots outta that."

"Best leave it behind, then. We've got knives, and I'm basically monsterproof."

"I wouldn't get too cocky," said Carl. "Those little asshole devils'll chew on anything."

They sat in silence for a couple minutes. Then the alarm pinged, and the tram turned a corner.

"Two minutes to the row seven nexus," she said. "We'll lose radio anytime now."

"Say, what's our itinerary for the rest of the day, assuming we can finish here in an hour or two?"

"Big if."

He chuckled. "Had to ask. I kinda lied about the heights thing. It's nothing I can't manage. Just, the less I'm thinking about it, the better."

Up ahead, they could see the dock lights of the row seven nexus, where catwalks and access tunnels branched out to the whole area.

"Well," said Shelly, "If we're finished in an hour and twenty-five, we'll go on to inspect two additional sites. Anywhere between that and four hours, we'll do just one more site. So most likely, we'll be home a little bit early and we'll be pushing a couple items onto the inspections backlog." The car rumbled to a stop, and the doors slid open. "Oh! And don't forget the softcovers for your boots. And a respirator just to be safe."

Carl nodded. "Coolant return line." The facility's coolant contained a bitterant that also gave it an unmistakable odor. Unpleasant normally, noxious at return line temperatures.

Nexus seven was further away from the noise of pumps and machinery, a background hum that was quickly tuned out by the listener. The result was a sense of emptiness not to be found at the worksites.

"Eerie. I'd kill for some background music."

"There's a portable speaker in the supply chest," said Shelly. "But we'll have to leave it in the nexus, or it'll give away our movements. Also, I kind of only have oldies onboard. How do you feel about Dolly Parton?"

"Greesh. Country music from this millennium is awful, but *Dolly* is immortal."

So, they set the little speaker on its telescoping tripod down in the center of the nexus, set a volume Shelly hoped would still reach them albeit faintly, and started it up. The intro to "Nine to Five" began to play.

"Shelly, you have great taste."

They set out on the southeast catwalk, where a faintly glowing sign read "To junction access." Carl went first, holding the laser rifle, with Shelly in the rear carrying the conduit repair kit. Thanks to the softcovers, they could move in near total silence.

It was about 30 meters to the next landing, where the walkway veered to the south for another 15, and branched off to walkways going left and right around the walled enclosure of the return artery and inspection access. So far, the music of Mrs Parton still dominated, but they could hear the faint hum of circulators growing louder. She was a comfort in the near-silence of Niantica's understructure. But soon, they would have to take what solace they could from the music of the facility itself.

Off in the direction of the access, they heard a distant screech. Carl sighted the laser, which had been retrofitted with a night vision scope, and peered through the darkness ahead.

"Nothing yet, " he said under his breath. "Motherfuck, I hope the little ones aren't mobile yet. I hear they're even tougher to hit."

"What I wouldn't give for wireless," said Shelly. "Mani's a crackshot with a rifle."

"Where's the network node?"

"Also through that archway, so, no good. We're runnin blind, Technician. Which means?"

"Aim carefully?"

"It *means*, no heroics. We withdraw at the first sign of danger. And I'll take point."

They advanced at an achingly slow pace, perhaps ten meters a minute, and as they passed under the archway into the junction, Carl caught the stench of coolant. As quickly and quietly as possible he slipped on the respirator. Coming out of the narrow into an open space with a 5 meter ceiling, he stopped short and laid a hand on Shelly's shoulder. Wordlessly he pointed up at the wall overhead, just left of the archway.

An enormous bat-like creature was hanging inverted by its meter-long tail, hooked onto 10 cm of black conduit pipe, snoring. The pipe's dangling wires were partially exposed, along with the broken-off corner of a circuit board.

The fucking network node had been torn away for a karyak perch.

He motioned to Shelly, and they pressed forward another meter or so into the dark cavern of the junction access. Then he knelt, shouldered the laser cutter, turned the dial for a split-second pulse that would easily burn a hole through its target, sighted, and took the shot.

He winced as the creature gave out a momentary pained squeal before dropping. While marksman was nowhere in his job description, he'd logged substantial time on the range with this very scenario in mind—from six meters, by night vision, dead center of the chin where it would vaporize the brain stem and larynx, bringing the beast down silently.

Instead, his shot had gone wide by half an inch, meaning it destroyed major arteries and damaged the spine, but not enough to prevent the creature crying out with what air remained in its lungs. The karyak plummeted to a narrow ledge, where it landed face down, legs spread, balls in full view.

"Shit!" He hissed, muffled slightly by the mask. "Not the mama."

"Not the mama," agreed Shelly.

Carl whirled, expecting an unpleasant surprise. Sure enough, the brood mother must've been lurking in the rafters, and here she came, swooping down. She was big even for a brood mother; those images with her back turned and wings folded didn't do her justice. Bearing down on them, Carl could see she had the armspan of a full grown man, and a slash of rust-colored fur across her bulging pectoral muscles.

A matriarch.

He was a lousy shot against moving targets, so he immediately wasted two. The gauge now read 67%. He was trying to line up another when Shelly put a hand to his chest, pushing him back, and her other arm up in front of her, brandishing a knife.

"Get down, ya dumb motherfucker!" she said. Then the brood mother was upon her, feinting and swooping and letting out shrieks of fury. The blade was a blur in her capable hands, but the clever karyak managed to stay out of its reach. "Come git some. Run, Carl, run!"

"Nuts to that. You kill the bitch, I've got your back."

Dutifully he knelt behind his durable companion and checked their six. Nothing within eyeshot, but he could hear the faint clattering of claws on metal, in numbers he couldn't possibly swear to. Perhaps running would have been advisable.

"Babies incoming! Maybe twenty meters out."

Carl turned back just in time to see the matriarch tear a ribbon of derma off Shelly's forehead. The robot hissed.

"That all you got, bitch?"

He had enough time that he could possibly have taken another shot; but the matriarch was hell on wings, and there wasn't a clear enough line of sight. And two big scary males were winging in now from down the corridor in either direction to back her up.

Carl waited patiently for his moment. Once the target had settled into a hover behind its lover, he squeezed the trigger. There was a dazzling blast of blue light. A perfect killshot. The big karyak male dropped straight down into the blackness.

He whirled about as the clattering grew louder.

Then came the torrent of juvenile karyaks around the bend, upwards of a dozen, small and flightless and terrifying. They were on the straightaway. So Carl bagged one, two, three, and then a fourth he only got on the shoulder. It stopped in its tracks, hissed, licked its wound, and surged ahead. As it leapt for his torso he swung the weapon down. It broke the juvenile's jaw with a harsh CRACK, and sent it skittering off into the abyss.

He let the laser cutter clatter to the floor and pulled his long knife, simultaneously bringing up his boot to kick at a fifth youngster. It ducked away. Then leapt up into the embrace of cold steely death.

"Shelly! Status!" he screamed as he flung it, too, away into the blackness. His eyes remained peeled for what he could hear approaching.

"More males, Carl. The matriarch's got a whole clan of lovers at her call!"

Presently a big one came charging around the corner toward him, hot on the heels of what had to be its progeny. It bellowed and surged ahead, then surprised him by coming in low, and sank its teeth into his thigh.

Carl howled, and drove his knife into the karyak's back twice, but it was latched on tight. His legs buckled and he landed on his ass, kicking feverishly to free himself. But all that got him was a second bite on the shin. In the tumult his gas mask came free. Unfortunately, his hands were both busy fending off the beast and two of its spawn. One bit his glove, and sailed off over the edge when the glove came free. Another was on top of him, trying to get at his nose. But the toxic stench got there first, and he turned and retched onto the catwalk..

From just above him came the visceral crunch of the little one's neck breaking. "Hang in there, Carl!"

With her back turned to the other males, Shelly brought her titanium fists down onto either side of the daddy karyak's skull with tremendous force and a wet thud. It squealed, released its grip, and staggered back, the sum of its wounds finally setting in.

"Mask up, cowboy!"

It was all he could do to slide the respirator back into place and not vomit in it. Then he sat up, and as his head cleared slightly, took stock of the situation.

Shelly had taken out several large males, including his. It'd cost her quite a bit of derma, and the matriarch seemed still hungry for more. Youngsters bit fruitlessly at her ankles, although some of them turned toward him as he grabbed the rails and tried to rise to his feet.

"Motherf—"

The room spun and he fell on his ass again.

"Carl, stay down! You've lost too much blood! Alright cunt, let's end this."

From his seated position, he had a front row view as Shelly waited for her moment, and with a blur of lightning-fast myomer contraction, flung the knife. It was a gambit, but it paid off.

Blood blossomed from the matriarch's chest. With a terrible scream, she lost altitude. She tried to make it to the walkway to land, but fell short, and tumbled out of sight.

Carl's head swam and he fell back onto the platform. For a while, he couldn't clearly make out sight or sound, just a drowned murmur like he was hearing the fight from underwater, and the sensation of weight as one or more pups climbed over him and were kicked away. The need to vomit resurfaced. He fumbled to pull off his mask, sicking up directly over the ledge and into the understructure. Then he blacked out.

When Carl came to, it was dim, and it took a minute to recognize that he was on the tram car's back cot. All the lights were off, save for a portable spotlight pointed down at his lower half. He smelled disinfectant, felt the faint buzz of painkillers, and the sting from the enormous, ragged, bandaged up gashes on his shin and thigh. Shelly had cut away the whole right pant leg.

There was a catheter going into his right wrist, and overhead he thought he saw a cluster of small IV bags and a tiny portable autopump.

"Muh. Huh. Um. Shelly?"

There was a few moments' silence, and then the car's intercom clicked to life. "Oh, good, Carl, you're up! Don't move. I'll be right with you, darlin." A few moments later he heard clanging on the walkways, and then the door shooshed open.

"We're all set to go, sug. I got the patch job done on the junction. It's a sixty second kludge but it'll hold until they come out to fix the network node... Hi there!"

Shelly's uniform was full of holes. Much of the right half of her face, along with her right forearm and patches of exposed torso, had had the derma-chroma layer bitten or clawed off, exposing the fascia of woven composite and allowing a few stray green indicator LEDs to shine through. Her smile however was mostly intact.

Carl tried to sit up, then winced and gave it up as the headache and queasiness came rushing back.

"Whoa, there, take it easy, soldier."

He gestured vaguely overhead. "Standard wound kit?"

"For you, the *advanced* wound kit. Plasma, ringers, tramadol, anti-bac, anti-emetic, epoetin. You fought valiantly, Carl, and I appreciate it. But you shoulda run. I did say no heroics."

Carl took a deep breath. "Am I gonna be in trouble with Al?"

Shelly chuckled, and braced herself slightly as the tram car unlatched and accelerated away from nexus seven. "Shit, no, that's my private assessment for your edification. All Mr Powatan needs to know is one, you're a gotdang hero, and two, we need a serious karyak extermination campaign. The bastards are gettin wise to our eyes and ears. *And* they're more social than we've seen before—inspection teams can't be expected to deal with entire clans."

The tram's intercom clicked on again, and out came Mani's round Bostonian voice. "Welcome back to the network, folks! ...Looks like I missed a *lot*. I'm rerouting you to medbay 2 and preparing a Medi unit. Pleasant dreams, Carl."

"What does he mean, pleasant dreeeeams?" said Carl. His head suddenly became even heavier, and the room went dark again.

Once or twice, he came around and could see, through tunneled vision, the ceiling overhead, and Shelly's battered face watching him placidly. He felt her hand on his; it was pockmarked from bites.

Finally, he came to in a different room altogether. This one had the bright lights and soft pastel tones of an ER, and sure enough, he heard the slow click of a standard autopump and the regular bip of a vitals receiver. The transmitter was in a little wristlet on his left hand.

"Can I..."

"Sit up?" Came the chipper and subtly breton voice of a Medi unit. "Of course, Technician Lemming."

He did, and this time his head only faintly ached. Medi came over and ratcheted up the bed for him, and he scooted back until he was flush against it.

"Shelly?" asked Carl.

"Oh, I'm afraid the unit who accompanied you has already headed off for decommission. She sends her love and best wishes. Now, how do you feel, sir?"

"Better. You know me, Medi, you can call me Carl."

"Of course, Carl. I do not share your complete personnel session data from your primary care Medi unit, but I will note it in your file. Are you still feeling nauseous?"

"Thankfully, no."

"And your leg?"

"It aches."

"Fine, fine. I'd like to keep you another hour for observation, then send you home in a mobi-chair. Aside from transfers, you should stay off of that leg for the next twenty-four hours. Do you anticipate any problems with household accessibility? Good, good. The facility will also be providing a home health aid for the next five to ten days. In the meantime, you have a visitor."

A bot peeked its head around the corner. Could that be...

"Hiya, hon!" said Shelly with a smile.

This unit looked a bit different—lighter skin, fewer freckles, dirty blonde hair and brown eyes—but the voice and demeanor were unmistakable.

"Hi, Shelly. C'mon in."

"Excellent," said Medi. "If there are no further questions, I will take my leave for now." Carl waved him off, and he turned for the door, passing the Shelly on her way in. She came around to the bedside and sat.

"I know," she said, "I've changed it up a bit. This unit was already in the area, so I swapped hosts and sent the other one to decom/recom."

"I'm sorry you got all torn up. Is it serious?"

Shelly shot him a pained look. "This is, I gotta say, one drawback to promiscuous Shelly. We have rapport, we're a great team, but then it's too easy for you to forget what I am. Carl, I wasn't damaged at all! What got tore up was the androidform, which is *replaceable,* and even then, it was far from totaled. The unit'll be back in service in a week, tops."

"Did it hurt?"

She sighed. "A fair question, I guess, since we've gotten all intimate and philosophical. Yes and no. We don't have true nociception, but we have pressure and temperature and integrity sensors. I gave myself a *notion* of pain, in order to be a more responsive lover. But I can easily ignore it. Or even enjoy it."

She leaned closer, and said with a wink, "A fact you'd have found out last night, if sadism happened to be part of your sexual proclivities, sug."

"Fair enough," he said. "Anyway, you were right, and I'm sorry. I went in too hot today."

The bot smiled, bent over and kissed his cheek.

"I don't fault you, Carl. It was a split second decision, and like I said before, it's not in my purview to give orders to techs. I do, however, hope that we can build on this experience, and next time, you'll trust me enough to follow my lead."

Carl grinned. "I will."

"Good. Remember, Carl, I am not like other girls. I can re-instantiate. Eve won't bat an eye if she has to pay for a new androidform cause I got wrecked while defending my team. Speaking of which... she wanted me to tell you, a little comp package has been transferred to your account."

"Oh?"

"Yep. A week's vacation and fifty thousand creds."

Carl's eyes went wide. "Fifty? That's not a little comp, it's more than my quarterly stipend!"

Shelly just laughed.

"It's standard for this tier of injury comp. We're also sending you a *me* for the next week. When I appropriated Medi's field medic expert knowledge, I also got home care. What'cha think about that, cowboy?"

Carl's cheeks and ears got hot again. "You mean..."

"Yes. I mean Nurse Shelly will be at your call, to do whatever it takes to repay your reckless bravery, and make recovery a bit less dull." Through the hospital gown she teased his gradually stiffening cock with a fingertip.

Under her breath she whispered, "Even if I have to restrain you for your own good."

Abruptly she stood, and glanced at the door. "I just remembered, they'll be expecting this unit back any time now. Tah-tah, sug! See you this evening!"

Carl shivered and tugged his blankets up to his shoulders. He sighed to himself. ESI was proving to be interesting, almost too interesting.

ABOUT
EZRA OWAIN

A bit jockey by day, a man of eccentric tastes by night. I've always been enchanted by the power of text—it can command machines, it can convey complex ideas, it can evoke powerful human emotions. And, it can help us appreciate the profound *weirdness* of our existence.

I like telling stories about people having unexpected and transformative experiences. Collisions, moments of inspiration, reflected glimpses of self. That could mean sex, it could mean an encounter with the gods, or any number of other things.

Aside from SF/F and horror I write a fair amount of short realistic romance and smut. When I'm not writing or coding, I can usually be found at home with my wife, cooking, reading, or buried under a pile of cats and dogs.